Meg Cabot is the author of the phenomenally successful The Princess Diaries series. With vast numbers of copies sold around the world, the books have topped the US and UK bestseller lists for weeks and won several awards. Two movies based on the series have been massively popular throughout the world.

Meg is also the author of the bestselling Airhead trilogy, *All-American Girl*, *All-American Girl: Ready or Not*, *How to Be Popular*, *Jinx*, *Teen Idol*, *Avalon High*, *Tommy Sullivan Is a Freak*, The Mediator series and the Allie Finkle series as well as many other books for teenagers and adults. She and her husband divide their time between New York and Florida.

Visit Meg Cabot's website at
www.megcabot.co.uk

The Princess Diaries

Sixsational

Meg Cabot

MACMILLAN

First published in the UK 2004 by Macmillan Children's Books

This edition published 2007 by Macmillan Children's Books
a division of Macmillan Publishers Limited
20 New Wharf Road, London N1 9RR
Basingstoke and Oxford
Associated companies throughout the world
www.panmacmillan.com

ISBN 978-0-230-76799-7

1 3 5 7 9 8 6 4 2

A CIP catalogue record for this book is available from
the British Library.

Typeset by Intype Libra Ltd
Printed and bound by CPI Group (UK) Ltd, Croydon, CR0 4YY

For Benjamin

Many thanks to Jennifer Brown, Beth Ader, Sarah Davies, Michele Jaffe, Laura Langlie and especially Benjamin Egnatz.

'She will be more a princess than she ever was – a hundred and fifty thousand times more.'

A Little Princess
Frances Hodgson Burnett

Albert Einstein High School Fall Semester Course Schedule for:

Student: Thermopolis, Amelia Mignonette
Grimaldi Renaldo, HRH Princess

Sex: F **Yr:** 10

Period:	Course:	Teacher:	Room:
Homeroom		Gianini	110
Period 1	PE	Potts	Gym
Period 2	Geometry	Harding	202
Period 3	English	Martinez	112
Period 4	French	Klein	118
Lunch			
Period 5	Gifted and Talented	Hill	105
Period 6	US Government	Holland	204
Period 7	Earth Science	Chu	217

Dear Students and Parents,

Welcome back from what I hope was a relaxing and yet intellectually stimulating summer vacation. The faculty and staff of AEHS look forward to spending another exciting and fruitful academic year with you. With this in mind, we'd like to share these few conduct reminders:

Noise

Please note that Albert Einstein High School is located in a residential – albeit vertical – community. It is important to remember that sound travels up, and that any excessive noise – especially on the steps at the front entrance of the school – which might be disruptive to our neighbours will not be tolerated. This includes shouting, screaming, shrill or explosive laughter, music and ritualistic chanting/drumming. Please be respectful of our neighbours and keep the noise level to a minimum.

Defacement

Despite what is often cited as Albert Einstein High School 'tradition' on the first day of classes, students are expressly forbidden from defacing, decorating or otherwise tampering with the lion statue, frequently referred to as 'Joe', outside the East Seventy-fifth Street entrance of the school. Twenty-four-hour surveillance cameras have been installed, and any student caught defiling school property in any way will be subject to expulsion and/or fines.

Smoking

It has been brought to the attention of this administration that, last year, large numbers of cigarette butts were daily swept up from the front steps of the Seventy-fifth Street entrance. In addition to the fact that smoking is strictly prohibited on school grounds, cigarette butts constitute a visual eyesore, as well as a fire hazard. Please note that any students caught smoking – either by a staff member or on the new video-surveillance cameras – will be subject to suspension and/or fines.

Uniforms

Please note that this year's standard AEHS uniforms include:

Female students:	*Male students:*
Long or short-sleeved white blouse	Long or short-sleeved white shirt
Grey sweater or sweater vest	Grey sweater or sweater vest
Blue-and-gold plaid skirt (or) grey flannel trousers	Grey flannel trousers
Blue or white knee-highs or blue or black tights or nude-coloured pantyhose	Blue or black socks
Blue-and-gold plaid tie	Blue-and-gold plaid tie
Navy-blue jacket	Navy-blue jacket

Please note that the wearing of shorts – including regulation gym shorts or athletic team uniform shorts – beneath skirts is prohibited.

Remember, classes commence the day after Labor Day, Tuesday, September 1, at 7:55 a.m. As always, tardiness will not be tolerated.

Welcome back!

Principal Gupta

Monday, August 31, Labor Day

WomynRule: Did you SEE it??? Did you get that hypocritical piece of garbage she sent out last week? Just who does she think she's kidding with that? You so know that that part about ritualistic chanting was directed at ME. Just because I organized a few student rallies last year. Well, we're going to show her. She might think she can stifle the voice of the people, but the student body of Albert Einstein High is NOT going to be intimidated.

>

FtLouie: Lilly, I—

>

WomynRule: Did you see that part about the surveillance cameras???? Have you ever HEARD of anything so fascist? Well, she can install all the surveillance cameras she wants, but that's not going to stop ME. It's just another example of how she's slowly turning this school into her own academic dictatorship. You know they used surveillance cameras in Communist Russia to keep the proletariat in line? I wonder what she'll bring in next. Ex-KGB militia, perhaps, as hall monitors? I so wouldn't put it past her. This is a total invasion of our right to privacy. That's why this year, POG, we're taking matters into our own hands. I have a plan—

>

FtLouie: Lilly—

>

WomynRule: —that will totally undermine her attempts to strip us of our sense of self and bend us to her will. Best of all, it's in complete compliance with school ordinances. When we're through, Mia, she won't even know what hit her.

>

FtLouie: LILLY!!! I thought the whole point of Instant Messaging was so that we could TALK.

>

WomynRule: Isn't that we're doing?

>

FtLouie: YOU are. I'm TRYING to. But you keep interrupting.

>

WomynRule: Fine. Then go ahead. What do you want to say?

>

FtLouie: I can't remember now. You made me forget. Oh, here's one thing: Stop calling me POG!

>

WomynRule: SORRY. God. You know, ever since that

```
            little brother of yours was born,
            you have got way . . . sensitive.
>
FtLouie:    Excuse me. I have ALWAYS been sens-
            itive.
>
WomynRule:  You can say that again, BL. Don't
            you want to hear my plan?
>
FtLouie:    I guess so. Wait a minute. What's BL?
>
WomynRule:  You know.
>
FtLouie:    No, I don't.
>
WomynRule:  Yes, you do . . . baby-licker.
>
FtLouie:    STOP IT!!! I AM NOT A BABY-LICKER!!!
>
WomynRule:  R 2. Just like the red panda.
>
FtLouie:    Just because I didn't think it was
            appropriate for my mother to take
            her six-week-old newborn on a peace
            march across the Brooklyn Bridge
            does not make me a baby-licker!!!!
            ANYTHING could have happened dur-
            ing that march. ANYTHING. She could
            have tripped and accidentally
            dropped him and he might have
            bounced off the safety railing and
            fallen hundreds of feet into the
            East River and drowned . . . if the
```

fall didn't crush all his little bones to pieces. And even if I dived in after him we might both have been swept out to sea by the current . . . OH, THANKS, LILLY!!! Why did you have to remind me????

>

WomynRule: Remember what the zookeeper had to do to the red panda?

>

FtLouie: SHUT UP!!!! NO ONE IS GOING TO TAKE AWAY MY BABY BROTHER BECAUSE I LICK HIM TOO MUCH!!! I HAVE NEVER ONCE LICKED ROCKY!!!!

>

WomynRule: Yes, but you have to admit you are a little obsessive-compulsive about him.

>

FtLouie: Well, SOMEBODY has to worry about him! I mean, between my mother wanting to lug him around to all sorts of inappropriate venues such as anti-war rallies — sometimes even taking him there on the SUBWAY, which you know is just a breeding ground for germs — and Mr G tossing him into the air and causing his head to smack against the ceiling fan, I frankly think Rocky is LUCKY to have a big sister like me who looks out for his welfare, since God knows no one else in the family is doing it.

>

WomynRule: Whatever you say . . . baby-licker.

>

FtLouie: SHUT UP, LILLY. Just tell me your
            stupid plan.

>

WomynRule: No. I don't want to now. I think
            you're better off not knowing.
            Baby-lickers like you, who worry
            too much, are probably better off
            not knowing things too far in
            advance, as it will just cause you
            to lick the baby harder.

>

FtLouie: Fine. I don't have time to hear
            your stupid plan anyway. Your
            brother's on the phone. I gotta go.

>

WomynRule: WHAT? Tell him to hold on. THIS IS
            IMPORTANT, MIA!

>

FtLouie: This may come as a surprise to you,
            Lilly, but talking to your brother
            is important too. At least to me.
            You know I've only seen him twice
            since I got back Friday—

>

Womynrule: I'm sorry I called you a baby-
            licker. Just wait one minute while
            I tell you—

>

FtLouie: —and once was dorm move-in day on
            Saturday, and hardly counts since

9

```
               he was all sweaty from carrying that
               mini-refrigerator  up   all   those
               stairs  after  the  elevators  broke
               down—
>
Womynrule:  MIA!!!  ARE  YOU  EVEN  LISTENING  TO
            ME????
>
FtLouie:    —and your parents were there and so
            was his Resident Adviser. And then
            on Sunday we went out, but I was
            still jet-lagged and I accidentally—
>
Womynrule:  I'M—
>
FtLouie:    —fell asleep while he was showing
            me his—
>
Womynrule:  GOING—
>
FtLouie:    —newest Magic deck, since Maya
            dropped his last one—
>
Womynrule:  TO—
>
FtLouie:    —and it got all mixed up with the
            decks he doesn't use any more—
>
WomynRule:  KILL YOU!
>
FtLouie:    terminated
```

10

Monday, August 31, Labor Day, 10 p.m., the Loft

Another school year. I know I should be excited. I know I should be thrilled at the prospect of seeing my friends again after having been on foreign soil for the past two months.

And I am. I *am* excited. I'm excited to see Tina and Shameeka and Ling Su and even – I can't believe I'm saying this – Boris.

It's just . . . well, it's going to be so DIFFERENT this year, with no Michael to pick up on the way to school and sit with at lunch and have drop by before Algebra – ACK! No Algebra this year either! Geometry! Oh, God. Well, I'll just think about that one later. Although Mr Gianini (FRANK. MUST REMEMBER TO CALL HIM FRANK) says people who do badly in Algebra always do really well in Geometry. Please, please let that be true.

And OK, it's not like Michael and I ever used to make out in front of my locker or anything, what with his lack of enthusiasm about PDA and my bodyguard and all.

But at least – because there was always a chance I could run into Michael in the hallway at any moment – I had something to look *forward* to at school.

And now, because Michael has graduated, there's *nothing* to look forward to. *Nothing*.

Except for the weekends.

But how much time is Michael even going to have to spend with me on weekends? Because he's in college now, and he has so much homework already there's no way we can see each other on week nights – not that, between princess obligations and my OWN homework, that was ever going to happen anyway. But still. It's like—

God, what is WRONG with my mother? Rocky was just crying there for like FIFTEEN MINUTES while she did absolutely NOTHING. I went out into the living room and there she was with Mr G, just sitting there watching *Law and Order*, and I was all, 'Hello, your son is calling you,' and Mom, without even looking up from the TV, was like, 'He's just fussing. He'll settle down and go to sleep in a minute.'

What kind of maternal compassion is THAT? Lilly can call me a baby-licker all she wants, but is it really any wonder I'm as maladjusted as I am if this is an example of how my mother treated *me* as a baby?

So then I went into Rocky's bright-yellow room and sang one of his favourite songs – 'Behind Every Good Woman' by Tracy Bonham – and he calmed right down.

But did anyone thank me? No! I walked out of his room and my mom actually looked at me (only because there was a commercial) and went, very sarcastically, 'Thanks, Mia. We're trying to get him to understand that when we put him down for the night he's supposed to go to sleep. Now he's going to think all he has to do is cry and someone is going to come in there and sing a song to him. I just got him over that while you were in Genovia this summer, and now we're going to have to start all over again.'

Well, EXCUSE ME! I may be a baby-licker, but is it really such a crime to have a little compassion for my only sibling? JEESH!

Let's see, where was I?

Oh, yeah. School. Without Michael.

Seriously, what is even the point? I mean, yeah, I know we're supposed to be going to school to learn stuff and all of that. But learning stuff was so much more fun when there was a chance of spotting Michael by the water fountain or whatever. And now I fully have nothing like that to look forward to until Saturday and Sunday. I'm not saying that life without Michael isn't worth living or whatever. But I will say that when he's around – or even when there's just a chance that he MIGHT be around – EVERYTHING is a lot more interesting.

The only bright spot in what appears to be a school year otherwise completely devoid of them, is English. Because it looks as if our teacher, Ms Martinez, might actually be enthusiastic about the subject. At least, if this note she sent around to all of us last month is any indication:

A letter to all members of Ms Martinez's Tenth Grade English Class:

Hello!

I hope you don't mind receiving a note from me before the new school year even starts, but as the newest teacher on the AEHS staff, I just wanted to introduce myself, as well as get to know all of you.

My name is Karen Martinez, and I graduated with a Masters in English Literature from Yale this spring. My hobbies include Rollerblading, tae-bo, visiting the many wonderful sights of New York City, and reading (of course!) literary classics such as Pride and Prejudice.

I hope to get to know each and every one of you this year, and to aid me in doing so, I'm asking that each of my students comes to our first class period with a previously prepared short bio as well as an expository writing sample (no longer than 500 words) on what you learned during your summer vacation – because, as you know, life's lessons don't discontinue during the summer months, just because school is not in session!

I'm sorry to be assigning homework before classes even begin, but I assure you that this will aid in my helping you to become the best writers you can be!

Thanks very much, and enjoy the rest of your summer!

Yours truly,
K. Martinez

Clearly Ms Martinez is extremely dedicated to her job. It's about time AEHS finally got some teachers who actually care about their students – Mr G excepted, of course.

Frank, I mean.

I am especially excited because Ms Martinez is the new adviser to the school paper, on which I am a staff member. I really feel, judging by how much Ms Martinez and I have in common – I really liked *Pride and Prejudice*, especially the version with Colin Firth, and I tried Rollerblading once – that I'm going to greatly benefit from her teachings. I mean, being an aspiring author and all, it's very important that my talent is appropriately moulded, and I already feel confident that Ms Martinez is going to be the Mr Miyagi to my Karate Kid – writing-wise. Not, you know, karate-wise.

Still, it's hard to figure out what to say in my bio, let alone my expository writing sample, on what I learned this summer. Because what am I going to write? 'Hello, my name is Amelia Mignonette Grimaldi Renaldo, HRH Princess. You might have heard of me, on account of there having been a couple of movies based on my life.'

Although to tell the truth, both of those movies took a lot of liberties with the facts. It was bad enough in the first one that they made my dad dead and Grandmere all nice and everything. Now, in the latest one, I supposedly broke up with Michael! Like *that*'s going to happen. That was entirely projection on the part of the movie studio – I guess to make the story more exciting or something. As if my life isn't exciting enough without any help from Hollywood.

Although I do have a lot in common with that

15

Aragorn guy from *The Return of the King*. I mean, we've both had the mantle of sovereignty thrust upon us. I would much rather be a normal person than an heir to a throne. I kind of got the feeling that Aragorn felt the same way.

Not that I don't love the land over which I will one day rule. It's just that it's really boring to have to spend the better part of your summer with your dad and your grandma when you'd LIKE to be spending it with your new baby brother, not to mention your BOYFRIEND, who is starting COLLEGE in the fall.

Not that, you know, Michael is going AWAY to college or anything, he's only going to Columbia, which is right in Manhattan, although it's way uptown, way further uptown than I usually go, except for that one time we went to Sylvia's for fried chicken and waffles.

Anyway, I wrote the following bio for Ms Martinez while I was still in Genovia last week. I hope that, when she reads it, she'll recognize in my prose the soul of a fellow lover of writing:

My Bio
by
Mia Thermopolis

My name is Mia Thermopolis. I'm fifteen, a Taurus, heir to the throne of the principality of Genovia (population 50,000), and my hobbies include being taught how to be a princess by my grandmother, watching TV, eating out (or ordering in), reading, working for AEHS newspaper, The Atom, *and writing poetry. My future career aspiration is to be a novelist and/or a rescue-dog handler (like when there's an earthquake, to help find people trapped under rubble).*

However, I will most likely have to settle for being Princess of Genovia (POG).

That was the easy part, really. The hard part was figuring out what to say about what I learned during my summer vacation. I mean, what DID I learn anyway? I spent most of the month of June helping Mom and Mr G adjust to having an infant in the house – which was a very difficult transition for them, since for so many years all inhabitants of our household were entirely bipedal (not counting my cat, Fat Louis). The introduction of a family member who will eventually – perhaps even for a year or more – get around mostly by crawling made me acutely aware of the entirely un-baby-safe

17

environment in which we live . . . although it didn't seem to bother Mom and Mr G so much.

Which is why I had to get Michael to help me install safety plugs in all of the sockets, and baby guards on all of our lower cabinet drawers – something Mom didn't entirely appreciate, since she now has trouble getting out the salad spinner.

She'll thank me one day, though, when she realizes that it's entirely because of me that Rocky hasn't got into any devastating salad-spinner accidents.

When we weren't busy baby-proofing the Loft, Michael and I didn't do much. I mean, there's lots of things a couple deeply in love can do in New York City during the summer: boating on the Lake in Central Park; carriage rides along Fifth Avenue; visiting museums and gazing upon great works of art; attending the opera on the Great Lawn; dining at outdoor cafes in Little Italy; et cetera.

However, all of these things can get quite expensive (unless you take advantage of student rates), except for that whole opera-in-the-park thing, which is free, but you have to get there at, like, eight in the morning to stake out your place and even then those weird opera people are all territorial and yell at you if your blanket accidentally touches theirs. And besides, everyone in operas always dies and I hate that as much as the blanket thing.

And while it's true that I am a princess, I am still extremely limited in the funds department, because my father keeps me on an absurdly small allowance of only twenty dollars a week, in the hope that I won't become a party girl (like certain socialites I could mention) if I don't have a lot of disposable income to spend on things like rubber miniskirts and heroin.

Although Michael got a summer job at the Apple Store in SoHo, he is saving all of his money for a copy of Logic Platinum, the music software program, so he can continue to write songs even though his band, Skinner Box, is on hiatus while its members scatter across the nation to attend various colleges and rehab clinics. He also wants Cinema HD, a twenty-three-inch flat-panel display screen, to go with the Power Mac G5 he's also hoping to buy, all of which he can get with his employee discount, but which all together will still cost as much as a single Segway Human Transporter, something I've been lobbying for my dad to buy me for some time now to no avail.

Besides, it's no fun to go on a carriage ride through Central Park with your boyfriend and YOUR BODY-GUARD.

So mostly when we weren't at my place installing baby guards, we spent June just hanging out at Michael's place, since then Lars could watch ESPN or chat with the Drs Moscovitz when they were not with patients or at their country home in Albany, while Michael and I concentrated on what was really important: making out and playing as much Rebel Strike as was humanly possible before being cruelly separated by my father on July 1.

Sadly, that grim day rolled around all too quickly, and I was forced to spend the latter months of the summer in Genovia, where I saved the bay (at least, if all goes as planned) from being overrun by killer algae that was dumped into the Mediterranean by the Oceanographic Museum in next-door Monaco (even though they deny it. Just like they deny that Princess Stephanie was driving the car when she and her mom went over that cliff. Whatever).

Which is what I ended up writing about. For Ms Martinez, I mean. You know, about how I surreptitiously ordered (and charged to the offices of the Genovian defence ministry) and then released 10,000 *Aplysia depilans* marine snails into the Bay of Genovia after reading on the Internet that they are the killer algae's only natural enemy.

I honestly don't know why everybody got so angry about it. That algae was strangling the kelp that supports hundred of species in the bay! And those snails are as toxic as the algae, so it's not like anything down there is going to eat them and break the existing food chain. They'll die off naturally as soon as their only source of nutrients – the algae – is gone. And then the bay will be back to normal. So what's the big deal?

Seriously, it's as if they think I didn't consider all this before I did it. It's almost as if people don't realize that I am not like a normal teen, concerned solely with partying and *Jackass*, but am actually Gifted, as well as Talented. Well, sort of.

I left out the part in my writing sample, though, about how everybody got so mad about the snails. Still, I just know Ms Martinez is going to be impressed. I mean, I used a lot of literary allusions and everything. Maybe, with her support, I might even get to write something other than the cafeteria beat on the school paper this year! Or start a novel and get it published, just like that girl I read about in the paper who wrote that scathing tell-all about the kids in her school, and now no one will talk to her and she has to go to school online or whatever.

Well, actually, I don't think I'd like that.

But I wouldn't mind not having to write about buffalo bites any more. J319.334

Oh no, Lilly is IM-ing me again. Doesn't she realize it is past eleven? I need to get my sleep in order to look my best for— **GALWAY COUNTY LIBRARIES**

Huh. I was going to say for Michael. But I won't even be seeing him at school tomorrow.

So what do I even care how I look?

```
FtLouie:    What do you want?
>
WomynRule: God, touchy much? Are you done talk-
           ing to my brother yet?
>
FtLouie:    Yes.
>
WomynRule: You two make me sick. You know that,
           don't you?
```

Poor Lilly. She and Boris went out for so long that she still isn't used to not having a boyfriend who calls to say goodnight. Not that Michael was going to bed yet when he called, but he knew I was. Michael doesn't have to get to sleep early, because even though he is taking eighteen credit hours this semester – so that he can graduate in three years instead of four and take a year off before he starts graduate school and I start college, so we can work together with Greenpeace at saving the whales – he purposely only chose classes that start after ten so he can sleep in.

You have to admire a man who is so good at planning ahead. I can barely even figure out what I'm going to have for lunch every day, so this is extremely impressive to me.

But Michael is an excellent planner. It would only have taken about half an hour to move him into his dorm at Columbia over the weekend (if the elevators hadn't broken down), because he had everything so organized. I went with the rest of his family to help, and to see what his room was like, and to, you know, see him for the first time since getting back from Genovia and all. I don't know how much Columbia charges for its student housing, but I wasn't very impressed. Michael's room is very cinderblocky, with a view of an airshaft.

Not that Michael even cares. All he was concerned about was whether it had enough data jacks. He didn't even look in the bathroom to see if it had one of those smelly vinyl shower curtains or the even smellier rubber ones (I looked for him: rubber one. Ew).

Guys are so weird.

I didn't meet his room-mate, because he hadn't moved in yet, but the sign on the door said his name was Doo Pak Sun. I hope Doo Pak turns out to be nice and not allergic to cat hair or anything. Because I plan on being in their room a LOT.

Still, I felt bad for Lilly, on account of her not having a one true love and all, so I thought I'd try to cheer her up.

```
FtLouie:    But it must be nice to have the apart-
            ment all to yourself now. I mean,
            isn't that what you always wanted?
            No Michael to drink all the Sunny D
            and eat all the Honey Nut Cheerios?

>
```

Womynrule: Whatever! Suddenly I have to do all
           MY chores AND Michael's too. And who
           do you think has to take care of
           Pavlov now?

>

FtLouie: Like Michael's not paying you.

>

Womynrule: Only twenty bucks a week. Hello, I
           worked it out, and that is only like
           a dollar a pooper-scooper-full.

>

FtLouie: TMI!!!!!!!!!!!!!

>

WomynRule: Whatever. I suppose you LOVE scoop-
           ing up after Fat Louie.

>

FtLouie: Fat Louie's poops are cute, just
           like he is. Same with Rocky's.

>

WomynRule: Um, NOW who is giving TMI, baby-
           licker?

>

FtLouie: I am choosing to ignore that. Hey,
           do you think the part in Dr Gupta's
           letter about not wearing shorts
           beneath your school skirt is
           because Lana always wore Josh's
           lacrosse uniform shorts under her
           skirt last year? You know, to show
           that Josh was her property?

>

WomynRule: I don't know and I don't care.
           Listen, about tomorrow—

```
>
FtLouie:   What?
>
Womynrule: Never mind. Sleep tight.
>
FtLouie:   ??????????????
>
Womynrule: terminated
```

Seriously. I can already tell that being a sophomore is not exactly going to be a picnic.

Tuesday, September 1, Homeroom

OH MY GOD.

So I thought it was going to be depressing to be back here. I mean, because school totally sucks anyway, but without Michael, it's REALLY going to suck.

And it *was* kind of sad to pull up in front of Lilly's building this morning and not see Michael there waiting for me, his neck all pinkly shaved. Instead there was just Lilly, not wearing any make-up and with her hair in 10,000 barrettes and her glasses on instead of contacts. Because now that Lilly has lost her one true love to another, she barely bothers to Make an Effort. Grandmere would be APPALLED.

And hello, I have even less reason than Lilly does to look good, but at least I washed my hair this morning. I mean, I still *have* a boyfriend, he's just going to another school. Lilly's the one who has yet to meet the man of her dreams.

Who is going to run from her the way people ran from the movie *Gigli* if she doesn't at least TRY to look a little more attractive.

But I didn't mention this to her, because it's not the kind of thing anyone wants to hear first thing in the morning.

Besides, as Lilly put it, we both have PE first thing. Why shower BEFORE PE when you're just going to have to shower again after?

Which is a good point.

Except that I think Lilly sort of regretted her decision not to bathe pre-PE when we stepped out of the limo in front of school and there was Tina Hakim Baba stepping out of HER limo. Tina was all, 'Oh my God!

It's so good to see you guys!', tactfully not mentioning anything about Lilly's glasses or hair. We were hugging when this guy walked up and at first I was like, *Whoa, hottie alert*, because even though I'm taken, I'm not DEAD, you know, and he was so big and tall and blond and everything . . .

. . . until he reached out and took Tina's hand and I realized he was BORIS PELKOWSKI!!!!!!!!!!!!!!!!

BORIS PELKOWSKI GOT HOT OVER THE SUMMER!!!!!!!

I know it sounds completely insane but there really is no other way to put it. Tina says Boris's violin teacher told him he'd have more stamina and play better if he started lifting weights, and so he did and he must have put on like thirty pounds of pure unadulterated muscle.

Plus he had laser surgery to correct his myopia so he wouldn't have to keep pushing up his glasses as he plays.

Also he got rid of his bionater and must have grown like two inches or maybe more, because now he's as tall as Lars and almost as wide in the shoulders.

Plus his hair has these blond highlights in it – Tina says from the sun in the Hamptons.

Seriously, it's like he got one of those *Queer Eye* makeovers or something.

Except they left out the part about not tucking his sweater into his pants. That's the only way I recognized him. Well, that and he still breathes from his mouth. Seriously, I was all, 'Hi, who are – BORIS?'

But MY astonishment was NOTHING compared to LILLY'S! She stared at him for like a whole minute after he was all, 'Oh, hey, hi, you guys.' – Even his VOICE has changed. It's sort of deeper now, like that kid's who plays Harry Potter in the movies.

When Lilly heard it, then turned around and recognized him, she kind of sucked in her cheeks . . .

. . . and just headed into school without a word.

But then when I saw her in the ladies' just before the bell rang, she'd put on some lipgloss and had slipped her contacts in and taken some of the barrettes out.

As soon as Lilly was gone I totally grabbed Tina and was all, 'OH MY GOD, WHAT DID YOU DO TO BORIS????' but in a whisper in her ear because I didn't want Boris to hear.

Tina swears she had nothing to do with it. Also, she said not to say anything in front of Boris about it, because he totally hasn't realized he's hot yet. Tina is trying to keep him from finding out about his new hotness because she's afraid as soon as he does he'll dump her for someone thin.

Except that Boris would never do anything like that because you can see the love-light for Tina shining in his eyes every time he looks her way. Especially now that he doesn't have those thick lenses.

Jeez! Who knew someone could change so much in just a couple of months?

Although, come to think of it, Tina might have a point, because with last year's senior class gone there are a LOT of totally gorgeous girls who are completely boyfriendless now. Like Lana Weinberger, for instance. Not that I think Boris would EVER go for Lana, but I totally saw her giving him the *Hey! Come over here* finger-crook by the water fountain before she figured out who he was and instead of crooking her finger, pretended to be sticking it down her throat like she was barfing at the sight of him.

So I guess SOME people haven't changed over the summer.

Shameeka says she heard that Lana and Josh are totally over. Apparently their love could not withstand the test of distance since Lana spent her summer at her family's house in East Hampton and Josh was in South Hampton, and the four miles between the two was just too much, especially with him leaving for Yale in the fall and thong bikini bottoms being very popular in Long Island this summer.

Excuse me. Four miles is nothing. Try 4,000. That's how far Genovia is from New York, and Michael and I still managed to see each other over the summer.

Poor, poor Lana. I feel so sorry for her. NOT. For the first time in my life, I have a boyfriend and Lana doesn't. It is unprincesslike to gloat over the misfortunes of others, but TEE HEE.

Another plus about Josh being gone is that I can actually get INTO my locker this year, since he and Lana aren't splayed up against it with their tongues in each other's mouths.

Although I do have to say that the guy who's been assigned Josh's old locker is pretty good-looking. He must be an exchange student because I've never seen him before. But he can't be a freshman because he's got razor stubble. At eight in the morning. Also, when he said, 'So sorry,' after accidentally sloshing some of his latte grande on to my boot while he was wrestling a gym bag into his locker, he fully had a South American accent, like that guy Audrey Hepburn was going to run off with in that movie *Breakfast at Tiffany's* before she came to her senses (or lost her mind, in Grandmere's opinion).

This is so BORING, sitting here, listening to announcement after announcement. There's an assembly this afternoon, so we've got an abbreviated seventh period. Who cares? Mr G (FRANK, FRANK) looks as tired as I feel. I swear, I love Rocky with every fibre of my being – almost as much as I love Fat Louie even – but the lungs on that kid! Seriously, he will NOT stop crying unless someone sings to him.

Which is OK during waking hours, because ever since I saw *Crossroads* I've been kind of worried, you know, about what I'm going to sing if I ever have to do karaoke to earn motel money on a road trip, and so Rocky's obsession with song gives me good opportunity to practise. I really think I've got 'Milkshake' down pat, and I'm working on 'Man! I Feel Like a Woman' by Shania Twain.

But when he starts up with the crying thing in the middle of the night . . . whoa. I love him, but even I, the baby-licker – which is SO not fair of her to call me, because I have NOT licked all of Rocky's fur off like that red panda on *Animal Planet* did to HER baby – just want to stuff a pillow over my head and ignore it.

Only I can't. Because everyone else in the loft is doing that. Because Mom's theory is that we're just spoiling him, picking him up and singing every time he cries.

But my theory is that he wouldn't cry if there weren't something wrong. Like what if his blanket has got wrapped around his neck and he's CHOKING???? If no one goes in to check, he could be DEAD by morning!

So I have to drag myself out of bed and sing the fastest song I know to him – 'Yes U Can' by Jewel – and then as soon as he dozes off, dive back into my own bed and try to fall back asleep before he starts up again.

OOOOH! My cellphone just buzzed! It's a text message from Michael!

GOOD LUCK 2DAY. LOVE, M

He got up early, just to wish me luck!!!! Could there BE a better boyfriend?

Tuesday, September 1, PE

I understand that obesity is epidemic in the US and all of that. I know that the average American is ten pounds heaver than their BMI says they should be, and that we all need to walk more and eat less.

But seriously, is any of that an excuse for forcing teenage girls to have to CHANGE CLOTHES, much less SHOWER, in front of one another? I so think not.

Like it's not enough that I even have to TAKE physical education. And it's not enough I have to take it FIRST THING IN THE MORNING. And it's not enough I have to STRIP DOWN IN FRONT OF VIRTUAL STRANGERS.

No, I also have to do it in front of Miss Lana Weinberger. Who also happens to have first-period PE.

And who took the liberty of pointing out in front of everyone, as we were changing into our gym clothes before class, that she 'really liked' my Queen Amidala panties – which I only wore for good luck on my first day back to class, although evidently they don't work any more – in a tone that suggested she did not like them at all.

And then she wanted to know if Genovia was suffering from an economic crisis, since its royals seemed to be shopping for their underwear at Target. As if all of us can afford to get our underwear from Agent Provocateur like Lana and Britney Spears!

I hate her.

Lilly told me not to worry about it . . . that Lana will be 'getting what she deserves' shortly.

Whatever that means.

Tuesday, September 1, Geometry

OK.
   I can do this. I can totally do this.

Converse:
The converse of a conditional statement is formed by interchanging its hypothesis and conclusion.

Contrapositive:
The contrapositive of a conditional statement is formed by interchanging its hypothesis and conclusion, then denying both.

Inverse:
The inverse of a conditional statement is formed by denying both its hypothesis and conclusion.

So:

Logically equivalent:

A conditional statement: a Æ b

The contrapositive of the statement: not b Æ not a

Logically equivalent:

The converse of the statement: b Æ a

Then inverse of the statement: not a Æ not b

I'm sorry. **WHAT?**

32

OK, once again I have managed to prove to be the exception to the rule. If people who are bad at Algebra are supposed to be good at Geometry then I should be the Stephen Freaking Hawking of Geometry, but guess what? I don't understand a WORD of this.

Plus Mr Harding? Yeah, could he BE any meaner? He already made Trisha Hayes cry over her isosceles triangles, and that's virtually impossible, since she's one of Lana Weinberger's cronies and also I'm pretty sure she's a female cyborg like in *Terminator 3*.

He's being totally nice to me, but that's just because one of his colleagues is my stepdad. Oh, and the princess thing, of course. Sometimes it actually doesn't hurt to have a six-foot-four Swedish bodyguard sitting behind you.

Tuesday, September 1, English

M - Could she be any cuter? - Tina

I know! When is the last time we had a teacher who wore anything that wasn't corduroy?

Totally! And her hair! That flippy thing it does on the ends!

That is so how I want my hair. So Chloe on *Smallville*.

I know! And her glasses!

Cat's eyes! With rhinestones! Could she be more Karen O?

Who's Karen O?

Lead singer for the Yeah Yeah Yeahs.

Oh right. I was thinking Maggie Gyllenhall.

I think it's Gylenhaal.

I think maybe it's Gellynhaal.

OH MY GOD, YOU IDIOTS, IT'S GYLLENHAAL! WOULD YOU TWO STOP PASSING NOTES AND FREAKING PAY ATTENTION? DO YOU WANT TO ALIENATE THE ONE TEACHER WHO ACTUALLY MIGHT TURN OUT TO BE ABLE TO TEACH US SOMETHING USEFUL????? — L

What's Lilly's problem today?

Um. I don't know, exactly. PMS?

Oh, sure. Anyway. So Maggie's brother's the one who went out with Kirsten Dunst, right?

RIGHT!

So cute!!!!!!!!!!

Oh, well. At least I have ONE good teacher. Ms Martinez is SO cool. It's so nice to have a teacher who is still close enough to our age to know about stuff like rubber spike bracelets and *The OC*.

As Ms Martinez was collecting our writing samples on how we spent our summer, she was like, 'And I just want you guys to know that you can come to me with questions about anything, not just English. I really want to get to know all of you as PEOPLE, not just as my students. So if there's anything – anything at all – you want to talk about, feel free to stop by. There is an open-door policy in my classroom, and I will always be here for you.'

Whoa! A teacher at Albert Einstein High who doesn't disappear into the Teachers' Lounge the minute class is over? Unbelievable!

Except I sort of wonder how long Ms Martinez is going to hang on to her open-door policy, because as I was leaving I noticed, like, ten people scurrying up to her desk to talk to her about their personal problems. Lilly was totally the first one in line.

I hope Ms Martinez counsels Lilly just to let the whole

Boris thing go. I didn't want to say anything to Tina, but her boyfriend's summer transformation into a hottie is fully why Lilly is wigging out today, not PMS, like I told Tina. It must totally suck to see the guy you dumped transforming into Orlando Bloom before your very eyes.

If Orlando Bloom had no fashion sense and breathed from his mouth, I mean.

I hope Lilly doesn't wear Ms Martinez out so much that she doesn't have time to read our writing samples tonight. Because I'm sure that when she's done with mine, she's going to want to submit it to a literary agent or something and get me a book deal. I realize fifteen is pretty young to have a multi-book deal with a major publishing house, but I've handled the princess thing pretty well so far. I'm sure I could handle a couple of book deadlines.

Euler diagram = relate two or more conditional statements to each other by representing them as circles

Tuesday, September 1, French

Mia — The new kid, second row from door, three seats down. Boy or girl? — Shameeka

Boy. He's wearing pants!

Hello. So am I. I forgot to shave my legs this morning.

Oh. OH.

Yeah. See what I mean?

Well, what's his/her name?

Perin. At least that's what Mademoiselle Klein said when she called roll.

Is Perin a boy's name or a girl's name?

I don't know. That's why I'm asking you.

Well, did Mademoiselle Klein say Per-run or Per-reen? Because if she's a girl, it would be Per-reen in French, right?

Yeah, but Mademoiselle Klein doesn't call role in French. She just said Perin, in English, with no accent.

So in other words . . . this is a mystery.

Totally. I just want to know whether or not to think he's cute.

OK. Here's what we'll do. We'll keep an eye on him/her, and see which bathroom he/she goes into before lunch. Because everyone goes to the bathroom before lunch, to put on lipgloss.

Not boys.

Exactly. If he doesn't go to the bathroom, he's a boy, and then you can like him.

But what if he's a girl who just doesn't wear lipgloss?

Argh! Mysteries are OK in books, but in real life they kind of suck.

Tuesday, September 1, Gifted and Talented

WHY? WHY, WHY, WHY did I think this year was going to be better – in spite of Michael not being around – than last year, just because at least Lana and Josh wouldn't be making out in front of my locker?

Because the thing is, when Josh was around, Lana was DISTRACTED and not actively seeking out targets to destroy.

But now that there's no man in her life, she has ample free time to torture me again. Like today at lunch, for instance.

It was all my fault in the first place for being greedy and going back to the jet line for a second ice-cream sandwich. Really, one ice-cream sandwich ought to be enough for a girl my size.

But there was something wrong with the three-bean salad. You would think with all the money the trustees invested in those surveillance cameras outside they'd have tossed just a LITTLE the cafeteria's way, so we could get something decent to eat in here beside frozen dairy products. But no. Lilly seems to have a point: apparently finding out who is stubbing their cigarettes out on Joe's head is more important than providing digestible sustenance for the student body.

So I was standing there waiting to get my ice-cream sandwich when I heard this voice behind me say my name and when I turned my head there was Lana and Trisha Hayes, who seemed to have recovered from Mr Harding's tongue-lashing – at least enough to join Lana in her quest to humiliate me publicly as often as possible.

'So, Mia,' Lana said, when I made the mistake of

39

turning around. 'Are you still going out with that guy? You know, that Michael guy, with the band?'

I should have known of course. That Lana wasn't trying to make up for all those years of being mean to me. I should have just put the ice-cream sandwich back and left the jet line then and there.

But I thought, I don't know, that maybe she was sorry for the whole underwear remark in the locker room that morning. I thought – don't ask me why – that maybe Lana really had changed over the summer too, just like Boris. Only instead of changing on the outside, Lana had changed on the inside.

I should have known something like that would be impossible, since in order to have a change of heart, Lana would actually have to HAVE a heart in the first place, and she obviously does NOT since when I said cautiously, 'Yeah, Michael and I are still going out,' she went, 'Isn't he in college now?'

And I said, 'Yeah. He goes to Columbia,' kind of proudly because, hello, at least MY boyfriend had chosen to go to a college in the same STATE as the one I live in, unlike Lana's ex.

'Well, have you two done it yet?' Lana wanted to know, as casually as if she were asking me where I'd got my highlights done.

And I was like, 'Done what?' Because I SWEAR I had no idea what she was talking about. I mean, who ASKS people things like that????

And Lana went, 'IT, you idiot,' and looked at Trisha and the two of them started laughing hysterically.

That's when I realized what she meant.

I swear I could FEEL my face turning red. Seriously. It must have turned as red as Lana's nail polish.

And then, before I could stop myself, I went, 'NO, OF COURSE NOT!' in a very shocked voice.

Because I WAS very shocked. I mean, this is a topic I barely discuss with my best FRIENDS. I certainly never expected to be discussing it with my MORTAL ENEMY. In the JET LINE.

But before I had a chance to recover from my paralysing astonishment, Lana went on.

'Well, if you want to hang on to him, you'd better hurry up,' she said, while Trisha giggled behind her. 'Because guys in college expect their girlfriends to Do It.'

Guys in college expect their girlfriends to Do It.

That is what Lana said to me. In the JET LINE.

Then, as I stood there staring at her in total and complete horror, Lana poked me in the back and went, 'Are you going to buy that, or are you just going to stand there?' and I realized the line had moved up so that I was standing in front of the cashier with my ice-cream sandwich melting in my hand.

So I handed the cashier my dollar and went back to my table with Lilly and Boris and Tina and Shameeka and Ling Su and just sat there not saying anything until the bell rang.

And no one even noticed.

Guys in college expect their girlfriends to Do It.

Can this possibly be true? I mean, I have seen a lot of movies and TV shows where guys in college seem to expect their girlfriends to do it. Such as *Fraternity Life*. And MTV's *Spring Break*. And *Revenge of the Nerds*.

But the guys in those movies and shows had girlfriends that were in college too. None of them were going out with sophomores in high school. Who will shortly be flunking Geometry. Who happen to be

41

princesses of a small European principality. Who have six-foot-four bodyguards.

Oh my God, is Michael expecting to have SEX with me??? NOW????

Naturally I assumed we would have sex ONE DAY. But I thought ONE DAY was way, way in the future. As far into the future as the day we go out to sea together to stop those whaling ships for Greenpeace. I mean, we have only been to second base ONCE and that was at the prom and I'm pretty sure now it wasn't even on purpose and I didn't even FEEL anything because of my strapless bra having way too much metal in it.

Am I supposed to believe that all this time I have been supposed to be getting ready to DO IT? But I am NOT ready to DO IT. I don't think. I mean, I didn't even want Michael to see me in a BATHING SUIT this summer, let alone NAKED—

OH MY GOD!!!! Last night he asked me to come over on Saturday to see how he and Doo Pak have set up their dorm room!!!!

WHAT IF THAT WAS REALLY AN INVITATION TO COME OVER AND DO IT AND I DON'T EVEN KNOW IT BECAUSE I AM SO UNSKILLED IN THE WAYS OF LOVE?????

What am I going to do about this? Clearly I need to talk to someone. But WHO? I can't talk to Lilly, because Michael's her BROTHER. And I can't talk to Tina, because she already told me the most precious gift a woman can give to a man is the flower of her virginity and that's why she's saving herself for Prince William, who is only allowed to marry a virgin.

She says she will settle for giving her flower to Boris if the Prince William thing doesn't work out by the time our senior prom rolls around though.

I can't talk to my MOTHER about it, because she can barely concentrate on the things she's SUPPOSED to be concentrating on – like raising my baby brother – as it is, without the added distraction of her teenage daughter wanting to talk to her about sex.

Besides, I know what she'll do: she'll schedule an appointment with her gynaecologist. Excuse me, but EW.

And obviously I can't say a word to Dad, because he would just arrange to have Michael assassinated by the royal Genovian guard.

And Grandmere would just pat me on the head and then tell every single person she knows.

Who does that leave? I'll tell you who:

MICHAEL. I am going to have to talk to MICHAEL about having sex with MICHAEL.

What am I, NUTS??? I can't talk to a BOY about SEX!!!! Particularly not THAT BOY!!!!

WHAT AM I GOING TO DO????????????

Oh my God, I think I'm having a heart attack. Seriously. My heart is beating like a million times a minute and practically exploding out of my chest. I think I have to go to the nurse. I think I have to—

Mrs Hill just asked me if I'm all right. Since it's the first day of class, she is pretending like she actually intends to supervise us this year. She made us all fill out a form stating what our goal for the semester is. You know, in this class. I peeked at Boris's and he'd written, *To learn Antonin Dvořák's* Concerto Royale *by heart and win a Grammy like my hero, Joshua Bell.*

Frankly, I don't think that's a very realistic goal. But Boris is almost as hot as Joshua Bell now, so maybe it really is doable. If hotness counts to the Grammy judges.

I tried to peek at Lilly's goal, but she is being way secretive. She put her hand over her paper and went, 'Back off, baby-licker,' to me in a very rude way.

I doubt she would be so mean if she knew the intense emotional maelstrom currently swirling within me concerning the future of my relationship with her brother.

Since I didn't know what to put as my goal – I don't even know why I'm IN this class this semester – I just wrote down, *To write a novel, and to not flunk Geometry*.

I can't believe Mrs Hill noticed that I was having a heart attack. She never used to notice anything we did. Well, that's because she was always locked in the Teachers' Lounge. But still.

I told her I'm fine.

But the truth is, I don't think I'll ever be fine again, thanks to Lana.

Tuesday, September 1, US Government

THEORIES OF GOVERNMENT
DIVINE RIGHT:

Creation of government is divine intervention in human affairs. Religious and secular were interwoven. People were far less likely to criticize a government created by God.

In Christian civilization, kings maintained that with the blessing of the church, the monarch was the legitimate ruler.

(Um, hello, except in Genovia, where the king of Italy, not God, gave the throne to my ancestress Rosagunde because of her bravery in the field of battle. Or the bedroom, I guess, considering that's where she killed her people's mortal enemy, Alboin. It is good to know that at least one of my family members excelled in something bedroom-related, since I have a feeling I'm going to be sadly lacking in that area, as I don't even like to look at MYSELF naked, let alone permit anyone ELSE to look at me.)

John Locke, a seventeenth-century philosopher, opposed Divine Right. He and others said: Government is legitimate only to the extent that it is based on the consent of the people being governed.

(Ha! Good for you, John Locke! Psych on all you kings and pharaohs, going around saying GOD put you on the throne! IN YOUR FACE!!!!)

45

Tuesday, September 1, Earth Science

Great. As if my day hasn't been bad enough. Guess who I have to sit by in this class this semester? Well, let's see, what letter of the alphabet comes right before T? That's right, S. Kenny Showalter.

Seriously. Did I stumble into some bad karma today or WHAT?

Apparently, Boris isn't the only one who grew over the summer. Kenny also sprouted up a couple more inches. Except that Kenny doesn't appear to have been doing any sort of weight training. So he just looks like the Scarecrow from *The Wizard of Oz* instead of Legolas.

Minus the pointy ears, of course.

Unlike the Scarecrow, though, Kenny actually has a brain. So he remembers all too well that the two of us used to go out. And that I dumped him for Michael. Well, technically, Kenny dumped ME. A fact about which he seems all too eager to remind me. He just went, 'Mia, I hope you can put aside your personal feelings about me and allow us to work together in a professional manner this semester.'

I said I thought I could. The thing is, if I were still going out with Kenny, and Lana said something about him expecting me to DO IT with him, I'd have just laughed in her face.

But Michael is different.

The other thing is, what does Lana even know about college boys? I mean, she's never even gone out with one! She could be totally wrong about Michael. TOTALLY WRONG.

I wish I had thought of saying this to her back in the jet line.

Kenny just asked me if I intended to spend this semester writing in my journal during class and then expect him to do all the work like I did when we were lab partners in Bio last year. Excuse me. I think someone is rewriting history here. I did NOT write in my journal during class last year.

Well, OK, maybe I did. But Kenny OFFERED to do all the lab work for me. And write it up afterwards. I mean, he LIKES that kind of thing. And he's good at it too.

If everybody would just concentrate on their own personal strengths, the world would be a much better place.

I guess I'd better stop writing now or Kenny will think I'm taking advantage of him. And then maybe he will expect me to DO IT with him to make up for it. EWWWWWWWWWWWWWWWWWWWWW!!!!!!!!!!!!!!!

Orbital mechanics – systematic long-term changes
1. Shape of orbit not constant circle – extreme ellipse over 100,000 years
2. Angle of tilt of axis varies – wobbles from 22 degrees to 24 degrees 30 minutes over 48,400 years
3. Precession – 26,000 years

PE:	No Assignment
Geometry:	Exercises, pages 11–13
English:	Pages 4–14, Strunk and White
French:	*Ecrivez une histoire*
Gifted and Talented:	N/A
US Government:	What is the basis for Divine Right theory of gov.?
Earth Science:	Section 1, define perigee/apogee

Tuesday, September 1, Assembly

There really ought to be some kind of constitutional amendment to abolish high-school convocations. Seriously. While they are abolishing PE.

Because not only are they a huge waste of school resources (how many times can you sit and listen to some paralysed dude talk about how he wished he'd never driven drunk? Hello, we KNOW), but also I'm beginning to think convocations are just an excuse for teachers to take a break from teaching. I fully saw Mrs Hill sneaking a cigarette outside the gym doors just now. I guess the front of the school isn't the only place where we need surveillance cameras.

Any time you get 1,000 teens in one room together, you just know there's going to be trouble. Principal Gupta already had to yell at the varsity girls' lacrosse team for throwing Swedish fish at the kids from the Drama Club, who weren't even doing anything, for once. Except, you know, looking weird, with their dyed black hair and facial piercings.

And I saw a couple of members of the Computer Club sneak beneath the bleachers just now. They had expressions on their faces I can only describe as diabolical. I wouldn't be surprised if it turns out they're down there unpacking their killer robot and programming it to unleash a reign of terror upon the world.

Principal Gupta is telling us how happy she is to have us all back. Lilly's hand just shot up. Principal Gupta said, 'Not now, Lilly,' and just went right on talking. Lilly is now muttering to herself beside me.

Tina, on my other side, is playing hangman with Boris. So far she only has the letter E right and has already earned a head and body. The spaces are

$$\_\ \_\ \_\ \_\ \_\ \_\ \quad \_\ E\ \_\ \_$$

I can't believe she can't figure it out. But I'm not helping. Because what she does with her boyfriend is her own business. Just like what I do with MY boyfriend is MY own business. Or at least it WOULD be my business if, in fact, I was doing anything with him. Which I'm not. Which is apparently a huge problem, bound to lead to his breaking up with me for some college girl who WILL do it with him.

But why SHOULDN'T I Do It with him? People Do It all the time. I mean, I wouldn't be here if my mom and dad hadn't—

Oh, great, now I feel like barfing. Why did I have to think about that? My mom and dad Doing It. Ew. Ew ew ew ew ew ew. That's even worse than the thought of my mom and Mr G—

OK, now I'm TOTALLY going to barf. EWWWWW!!!!!!!!!!!

Now Principal Gupta is talking about the wonderful extra-curriculars that exist at Albert Einstein High, and how we should all really try to take advantage of them. Lilly put her hand up again, but Principal Gupta just said, 'Not now, Lilly.' Nobody else is paying any attention.

Tina got another letter. Now the spaces go

$$\_\ \_\ \_\ \_\ \_\ A\ \quad \_\ E\ \_\ \_$$

But Boris has added two arms to his hangman. Why doesn't Tina try the letter L? This is so aggravating.

Now Principal Gupta is introducing the different student groups, to show how many extra-curriculars AEHS has to offer. It turns out the other new guy who got assigned Josh's old locker and who spilt his latte on my boot is an exchange student from Brazil named Ramon Riveras. He is going to be on the soccer team.

That ought to make all the soccer moms very happy. Especially if after he wins, he whips off his shirt and swings it around his head the way Josh used to.

Ramon is sitting with Lana and Trisha and all the rest of the popular people. How did he know? I mean, he isn't even FROM this country. How could he know who the popular people even are, let alone that he's one of them and should sit with them? Is this something popular people are just born with? Something they know innately?

Now Principal Gupta is talking about Student Council, and how we should all be eager to join, and what a wonderful opportunity it is to show your school spirit, and how it also looks good on your transcript. She is almost making it seem as if anybody who wanted to could run for Student Council and win. Which is so bogus, because everyone knows only popular people ever win elections for Student Council. Lilly runs every single year and has never once won. Last year the person who beat her wasn't even smart. No, last year she got soundly defeated by Nancy di Blasi, captain of the varsity cheerleading team (Lana Weinberger's mentor in evil), a girl who spent way more time organizing bake sales so that the cheerleaders could get a well-deserved trip to Six Flags than she did lobbying for real student reforms.

'Do we have any nominations for Student Council

President?' Principal Gupta wants to know. Lilly's hand just shot up. Principal Gupta is ignoring it this time.

'Anyone?' Principal G keeps asking. 'Anyone at all?'

Tina just said to Boris, 'Um, gee, let me see. Is there a Y?'

'Oh for God's sake.' I can no longer help myself. Maybe it's the looming threat of defloration. Or maybe it's just that I don't get to play hangman during school hours with the love of my life any more. In any event, I went, 'It's JOSHUA BELL, OK? JOSHUA BELL!'

Tina's all, 'Ooooooh! You're right!'

Ramon Rivera is laughing at something Lana has whispered in his ear.

Lilly's waving her arm around like a crazy person. Hers is the only hand in the air. Finally, Principal Gupta has no choice but to go, 'Lilly. We discussed this last year. You can't nominate yourself for Student Council President. Someone has to nominate you.'

Lilly stands up, and out of her mouth come the words, 'I'm not nominating myself this year. I NOMINATE MIA THERMOPOLIS!!!'

Tuesday, September 1, in the limo on the way to the Plaza Hotel

Seriously. Why am I even friends with her?

Tuesday, September 1, the Plaza

First princess lesson of the new school year, and – thank God – Grandmere is on the phone. She just snapped her fingers at me and pointed at the coffee table in the middle of her suite. I went over there and found these faxes all over it – letters of complaint from various members of the French scientific community and Monaco's Oceanographic Museum.

Huh. I guess they're kind of mad about the snails.

Whatever! Like I don't have WAY bigger problems right now than a bunch of angry marine biologists. Hello – apparently, if I want to keep my boyfriend, I have to Do It. As if that's not bad enough, I've been nominated for STUDENT COUNCIL PRESIDENT.

I honestly don't know what Lilly was thinking. Could she REALLY have thought I'd just sit there and be all, 'Student Council President? Oh, OK. Sure. Because, you know, I'm only the heir to the throne of an entire foreign country. It's not like *I don't have anything else to do.*'

WHATEVER!!! I fully grabbed her arm and pulled it down and was all, *'LILLY, WHAT DO YOU THINK YOU'RE DOING????'* under my breath, since of course every single head in the entire gym had swivelled in our direction and everyone was staring at us, including Perin and Ramon Riveras and the guy who hates it when they put corn in the chilli, who I thought had graduated. But I guess not.

'Don't worry,' Lilly hissed back. *'I've got a plan.'*

Apparently, part of Lilly's plan was to kick Ling Su in the shin very very hard until she squeaked, 'Um, I do, Principal Gupta,' when Principal Gupta asked in a confused voice, 'Does, uh, anyone second that nomination?'

I couldn't believe this was even happening. It was like a nightmare, only worse, because that guy who hates corn in his chilli is never in my nightmares.

'But I—' I started to protest, but then Lilly kicked ME really hard in the shin.

'Ms Thermopolis accepts the nomination!' Lilly called down to Principal Gupta.

Who totally didn't look as if she believed it. But who went, 'Well. If you're sure, Mia,' anyway, without waiting for any response from me.

Next thing I knew, Trisha Hayes had jumped to her feet and was screaming, 'I nominate Lana Weinberger for Student Council President!'

'Well, isn't that nice,' Principal Gupta said, when Ramon Riveras seconded Trisha's nomination of Lana, but only after Lana elbowed him . . . pretty hard, it looked like, from where I was sitting. 'Do any members of the junior or senior class care to enter a nomination? No? Your apathy is duly noted. Fine then. Mia Thermopolis and Lana Weinberger are your nominees for Student Council President. Ladies, I trust you'll run a good clean election. Voting will be next Monday.'

And that was that. I'm running for Student Council President. Against Lana Weinberger.

My life is over.

Lilly kept saying it's not. Lilly kept saying she has a plan. Lana running against me wasn't part of that plan – 'I can't believe she's doing that,' Lilly said as we were filing out of school after Assembly. 'I mean, she's only doing it because she's jealous.' – but Lilly says it doesn't matter, because everyone hates Lana, so no one will vote for her.

Everyone does NOT hate Lana. Lana is one of the

most popular girls in school. *Everyone* will vote for her.

'But, Mia, you're pure and good of heart,' Boris pointed out to me. 'People who are pure and good of heart always beat out evil.'

Um, yeah. In books like *The Hobbit*, for crying out loud.

And the fact that I'm so pure? That's probably why I'm about to lose my boyfriend.

And I think there are many historical examples of people who are very clearly NOT good at heart winning more elections than those that are.

'You're not going to have to lift a finger,' Lilly said as Lars handed me into the limo to Grandmere's. 'I'll be your campaign manager. I'll take care of *everything*. And don't worry. *I have a plan!*'

I don't know why Lilly thinks her constant assurances that she has a plan are in any way comforting to me. In fact, the opposite is true.

Grandmere just hung up the phone.

'Well,' she says. She's already on her second Sidecar since I got here. 'I hope you're satisfied. The entire Mediterranean community is up in arms about that little stunt you pulled.'

'Not everybody.' I found two or three very supportive faxes in the pile and showed them to her.

'Pfuit!' was all Grandmere said. 'Who cares what some fishermen have to say? They aren't exactly experts on the matter.'

'Yeah,' I said, 'but they happen to be *Genovian* fishermen. My countrymen. And isn't my first obligation to protect the interests of my countrymen?'

'Not at the expense of straining diplomatic relations with your neighbours.' Grandmere's lips are pressed so tightly together, they're practically disappearing. 'That was the President of France, and he—'

Thank God the phone rang again. This is pretty awesome. I'd have dumped 10,000 snails into the Genovian bay a long time ago if I'd had any idea doing so would get me out of having princess lessons.

Although it kind of sucks that everyone is so mad.

Jeez. I knew all about the French of course. But who knew marine biologists were so TOUCHY?

But seriously, what was I supposed to do, sit around and LET killer algae destroy the livelihoods of families who for centuries had made their living from the sea? Not to mention innocent creatures such as seals and porpoises, whose very survival depends on ready access to the kelp beds the *Caulerpa taxifolia* is totally strangling? Could anyone really imagine that *I* would allow an environmental disaster of those proportions to occur under my very nose, in my own bay – *me*, Mia Thermopolis? – when I knew of a way (albeit only theoretical) to stop it?

'That was your father,' Grandmere said, after slamming down the phone. 'He is extremely distraught. He just heard from the Oceanographic Museum in Monaco. Apparently some of your snails have drifted over to *their* bay.'

'Good.' I kind of like this environmentalist rebel thing. It keeps my mind off other stuff. Like that my boyfriend is going to dump me if I don't put out. And that I am currently running against the most popular girl in school for Student Council President.

'Good?' Grandmere jumped up out of her seat so fast she totally dumped Rommel, her toy poodle, off her lap. Fortunately Rommel is used to this kind of treatment

56

and has trained himself to land on his feet, like a cat. '*Good?* Amelia, I don't pretend to understand any of this – all this fuss over a little plant and some snails. But I would think you of *all* people would know that . . .' She picked up one of the faxes and read aloud from it. '. . . "When you introduce a new species into a foreign environment, total devastation can occur." '

'Tell that to Monaco,' I said. 'They're the ones who dumped a South American algae into the Mediterranean in the first place. All I did was dump a South American snail in after it to clean up THEIR mess.'

'Have you learned NOTHING that I've tried to teach you this past year, Amelia?' Grandmere wants to know. 'Nothing of tact or diplomacy or even SIMPLE COMMON SENSE?'

'I GUESS NOT!!!!'

OK, probably I shouldn't have screamed that quite as loudly as I did. But seriously, WHEN is she going to GET OFF MY BACK????? Can't she see I have WAY BIGGER THINGS to worry about than what a bunch of stupid FRENCH MARINE BIOLOGISTS have to say????

Now she's giving me the evil eye. 'Well?'

That's what she just said. Just, 'Well?'

And even though I know I'm going to regret it – how can I not? – I go, 'Well . . . what?'

'Well, are you going to tell me what's got you so frazzled?' she wants to know. 'Don't try denying it, Amelia. You are as bad at hiding your true feelings as your father. What happened at school today that's got you so upset?'

Yeah. Like I'm really going to discuss my love life with Grandmere.

Although I have to say that the last time I did this – with the whole prom thing – Grandmere gave me some pretty kick-ass advice. I mean, it got me to the prom, didn't it?

Still, how can I tell my GRANDMOTHER that I'm afraid if I don't have sex with my boyfriend he's going to dump me?

'Lilly nominated me to be Student Council President,' I said, because I had to say SOMETHING or she'd hound me into an early grave. She's done it before.

'But that's wonderful news!'

For a minute, I thought Grandmere was actually going to kiss me or something. But I totally ducked and she pretended like instead she was going to lean down and pat Rommel on the head. Which is maybe what she meant to do all along. Grandmere is not a very kissy person. At least not with me. Rocky, she kisses all the time. And she is not even technically related to him.

I keep antibacterial wipes around for this very reason. To wipe Grandmere's kisses off Rocky, I mean. There is no telling where Grandmere's lips have been on any given day.

Anyway.

'It's not wonderful!' I yelled at her. Why am I the only person who sees this? 'I'm going to be running against Lana Weinberger! She's the most popular girl in the whole school!'

Grandmere swirled the swizzle stick in her Sidecar.

'Really,' she said thoughtfully. 'Interesting turn of events. There's no reason, however, that you shouldn't be able to defeat this Shana person. You're a princess, remember! What is she?'

'A cheerleader,' I said. 'And it's Lana, not Shana. And

believe me, Grandmere, in the real world – such as high school – being a princess is NOT an advantage.'

'Nonsense,' Grandmere said. 'Being a royal is ALWAYS beneficial.'

'Ha!' I said. 'Tell that to Anastasia!' Who, you know, got shot for being royal.

But Grandmere was totally not paying attention to me any more.

'A student election,' she was muttering to herself, looking far away. 'Yes, that might be just the thing . . .'

'I'm glad *you*'re happy about it,' I said, not very graciously. 'Because, you know, it's not like I don't have other things to worry about. Like I'm pretty sure I'm going to flunk Geometry. And then there's the whole thing with dating a college boy . . .'

But Grandmere was totally off in her own little world.

'What day are votes cast?' Grandmere wanted to know.

'Monday.' I narrowed my eyes at her. I'd wanted to throw her off the Michael scent, but now I wasn't so sure this had been such a good idea. She seemed WAY too into the election thing. 'Why?'

'Oh, no reason.' Grandmere leaned over, scooped up all the snail faxes, and dropped them into the ornate gilt trash can by her desk. 'Shall we proceed with your lesson for the day, Amelia? I believe a little brushing up on our public-speaking techniques might be in order, given the circumstances.'

Seriously. Is it not enough that I be burdened with a psychotic best friend? Must my grandmother be losing her mind AT THE EXACT SAME TIME????

Tuesday, September 1, the Loft

So as if this day hasn't been long enough, when I got home just now, it was to find utter chaos reigning. Mom was bouncing a screaming Rocky in her arms, tearfully singing 'My Sharona' to him, while Mr G sat at the kitchen table, yelling into the phone.

I could tell right away that something was wrong. Rocky hates 'My Sharona'. Not that I would expect a woman who took her three-month-old to a protest rally where someone ended up throwing a trash can through a Starbucks window to remember which songs he likes and doesn't like. But the 'M-m-m-my' part actually makes him spit up, if you accompany it with jiggling, as my mom was doing, and she seemed oblivious to the white stuff all over her back and shoulders.

'What's going on, Mom?' I asked.

Boy, did I get an earful.

'My mother,' Mom shouted above Rocky's screams. 'She's threatening to come here, with Papaw. Because she hasn't seen the baby.'

'Um,' I said. 'OK. And that's bad because . . .'

My mom just looked at me with her eyes all wide and crazy.

'Because she's my MOTHER,' she shouted. 'I do not want her coming here.'

'I see,' I said, as if this made sense. 'So you're—'

'—going there,' my mom finished, as Rocky's screaming hit new decibels.

'No,' Mr G was saying into the phone. 'Two seats. Just two seats. The third person is an infant.'

'Mom,' I said, reaching out and taking Rocky from her, careful to avoid the spit-up still spewing from his

60

mouth like lava from freaking Krakatoa. 'Do you really think that's such a good idea? Rocky's a bit young for his first plane ride. I mean, all that recycled air. Someone with Ebola or something could sneeze and next thing you know, the whole plane could come down with it. And what about the farm? Didn't you hear about all those school kids who got E. coli from that petting zoo in Jersey?'

'If it will keep my parents from coming here,' Mom said, 'I'm willing to risk it. Do you have any idea what kind of minibar bill they racked up the time your father put them up at the SoHo Grand?'

'OK,' I said, between verses of 'Independent Woman', which always has a soothing effect on Rocky. He is much more into R & B than rock. 'So when are we going?'

'Not you,' Mom said. 'Just Frank and I. And Rocky of course. You can't go. You have school. Frank's taking a vacation day.'

I knew it had sounded too good to be true. Not the potential risks to my little brother's health but, you know, that I might get to escape to Indiana instead of facing election hell back at school, and the potential break-up with my boyfriend.

Which reminded me.

'Um, Mom,' I said, as I followed her into Rocky's room, where she'd apparently been engaged in putting away his clean laundry before Mamaw's blow fell. 'Can I talk to you about something?'

'Sure.' Although my mom didn't exactly sound like she was much in the mood to talk. 'What?'

'Uh . . .' Well, she HAD told me once that I could talk to her about ANYTHING. 'How old were you the first time you had sex?'

I fully expected her to say, 'I was in college,' but I guess she was so busy trying to cram all of Rocky's *My Mommy Is Mad as Hell and She Votes* sleepsuits into his tiny dresser that she didn't think about what she was saying beforehand. She just went, 'Oh God, Mia, I don't know. I must have been, what, about fifteen?'

And then it was like she realized what she'd just said and she sucked in her breath really fast and looked at me all wide-eyed and went, 'NOT THAT I'M PROUD OF IT!!!'

Because she must have remembered at the same time I did that *I* am fifteen.

The next thing I knew, she was blathering a mile a minute.

'It was Indiana, Mia,' she cried. 'It's not like there was so much else to do. And it was twenty years ago. It was the eighties! Things were different back then!'

'Hello,' I said, because I've fully seen every episode of *I Love the Eighties*, including *I Love the Eighties Strikes Back*. 'Just because people wore legwarmers all the time—'

'I don't mean that!' Mom cried. 'I mean, people actually thought George Michael was straight. And that Madonna would be a one-hit wonder. Things were DIFFERENT then.'

I couldn't think of anything to say. Except, moronically, 'I can't believe you and Dad did it for the first time when you were FIFTEEN.'

And then, noticing my mother's expression, I was like, 'Oh my God. That's right!' Because she didn't even meet Dad until she was in college. 'MOM!!! Who WAS it?'

'His name was Wendell,' my mom said, her eyes

going all dreamy, either because Wendell had been a total hottie or because Rocky had finally quit crying and was instead drooling all over the lion patch on my uniform blazer, so that for once the loft was filled with blissful silence. 'Wendell Jenkins.'

WENDELL???? The man my mom gave the precious flower of virginity to was named WENDELL????

I seriously would NOT have sex with someone named Wendell.

But then I am having grave reservations about having sex with anyone, so my opinion probably isn't worth much.

'Wow,' my mom said, still looking dreamy. 'I haven't thought of Wendell in ages. I wonder whatever happened to him.'

'You don't KNOW?' I cried, loudly enough that Rocky kind of gave a little start in my arms. But he calmed down after a quick verse of Pink's 'Trouble'.

'Well, I mean, I know he graduated,' my mom said quickly. 'And I'm pretty sure he married April Pollack, but—'

'Oh my GOD!' This was shocking. No wonder Mom is the way she is! 'He was two-timing you????'

'No, no,' my mom said. 'He started going out with April after he and I broke up.'

I nodded knowingly. 'You mean he loved you and left you?' Just like Dave Farouq El-Abar and Tina Hakim Baba!

'No, Mia,' my mom said with a laugh. 'Good grief, Mia, you have an uncanny ability to turn everything into a country and western song. I mean, he and I went out, and it was great, but I eventually realized . . . well, I wanted out of Versailles and he didn't, so I left and he stayed. And married April Pollack.'

Just like Dean married that other girl on *Gilmore Girls*! Only he and Rory never, you know, Did It.

'But . . .' I stared at my mom. 'You loved him?'

'Of course I loved him,' my mom said. 'Gosh, Wendell Jenkins. I really haven't thought of him in ages.'

JEEZ! I can't believe my mother is not still in contact with the boy who relieved her of her virginity! What kind of school did she GO to back then anyway?

'Why are you asking me all these questions, Mia?' my mom finally wanted to know. 'Are you and Michael—'

'No,' I said, hastily shoving Rocky back into her arms.

'Mia, it's perfectly all right if you want to talk to me about—'

'I don't,' I said fast. Real fast.

'Because if you—'

'I don't,' I said again. 'I have homework. Bye.'

And I went into my room and locked the door.

There must be something wrong with me. I'm serious. Because you could totally tell, when Mom was remembering having sex with Wendell Jenkins, that she'd had a good time. Doing It. Everyone seems to have a good time Doing It. Like in movies and on TV and everything. Everyone seems to think Doing It is just, like, the pinnacle of experiences.

Everyone except for me. Why am I the only person who, when she thinks about Doing It, feels nothing but . . . sweaty? This can't be a normal reaction. This has to be yet another genetic anomaly in my make-up, like the absence of mammary glands and size-ten feet. I am totally lacking in the Do It gene.

I mean, I WANT to Do It. I mean, I *guess* that's what I want, you know, when Michael and I are kissing and

I smell his neck and I get that feeling like I want to jump on him. Surely this is an indication that I want to Do It?

Except that to Do It you actually have to take your CLOTHES OFF. In FRONT OF THE OTHER PERSON. I mean, unless you're one of those Hasidic Jews who do it through a hole in the sheet like Barbra Streisand in *Yentl*.

And I do not think I am ready to TAKE MY CLOTHES OFF in front of Michael. It is bad enough taking them off in front of Lana Weinberger in the locker room first thing in the morning. I don't think I could ever take them off in front of a BOY. Especially not a boy I am actually in love with and hope to marry someday, if he ever asks me and if I ever get over this whole not-wanting-to-take-my-clothes-off-in-front-of-him thing.

Although I definitely wouldn't mind seeing Michael with HIS clothes off.

Is this a double standard?

I wonder if my mom felt the same about Wendell Jenkins. She MUST have or she wouldn't have Done It with him.

And yet here she is, twenty years later, and she doesn't even know where he IS now.

Wait, I bet I could find him. I could do a Yahoo! People search!

OH MY GOD!!! HERE HE IS!!!! WENDELL JENKINS!!! I mean, there's no picture, but he works for...OH MY GOD, HE WORKS FOR THE VERSAILLES POWER COMPANY!!!! HE IS THE GUY WHO FIXES THE POWER LINES WHEN YOUR LIGHTS GO OUT BECAUSE OF A TORNADO OR WHATEVER!!!!

I cannot believe my mom gave the flower of her virginity to a guy who now works for the VERSAILLES POWER COMPANY!!!!!!!!!!!!!!!

Not that there is anything wrong with someone who works for a power company. It is no different than being a high-school Algebra teacher, I guess.

But at least Mr G doesn't have to wear a JUMPSUIT to work.

I wonder if April Pollack, the girl who became Mrs Wendell Jenkins instead of my mom, is on here.

OH MY GOD! She is!!!! APRIL POLLACK WAS ELECTED CORN PRINCESS OF VERSAILLES, INDIANA, IN 1985!!!!!!!!!!!

My mom Did It with a guy who later went on to marry a corn princess.

Which is very ironic, considering my mom later went on to have the illegitimate child of a prince! Hello, I wonder if Wendell even knows this. That his ex, Helen Thermopolis, is the mother of the heir to the throne of GENOVIA. I bet he wouldn't feel so good about having dumped her for Miss Corn Princess April if he knew THAT, would he????

Although I guess he didn't really dump her if it's true what my mom said about her and Wendell wanting different things.

Could this happen to me and Michael? Could we want different things someday? In twenty years will Michael be married, not to the Princess of Genovia but to some CORN PRINCESS????

AHHHHHHHHHHHHH!!!! SOMEONE IS IMing ME!!!! Who could it be NOW?

Help! It's Michael!

```
SkinnerBx: Hey!
```

Since going Mac, Michael's changed his IM address. It used to be LinuxRulz.

```
SkinnerBx:  How was your first day back?
```

Oh my God. He hasn't heard. Well, how WOULD he? It's not like he was there. Or like Lilly would tell him. Since they don't live together any more.

```
FtLouie:    It was . . . the usual.
```

Well, it WAS. My life is a constant roller-coaster . . . joy followed by crushing disappointments, with occasional patches where nothing at all happens and I just admire the scenery.

I figured I should change the subject.

```
FtLouie:    How was YOUR first day?
>
SkinnerBx:  Fantastic! Today in my Economics of
            Sustainable Development class the
            professor talked about how in the
            next ten to twenty years petroleum,
            the cheapest and most effective
            fuel on the planet — you know, what
            we use in cars and to heat our
            homes and in Chapstick and all —
            will run out. See, a hundred years
            ago, when petroleum was first dis-
            covered, the world population was
            only two billion. Now, with six
```

billion people — a population explosion almost directly caused by more easily accessible fuel — the earth cannot maintain that many people with the amount of petroleum it has left. Since the population isn't getting any smaller, oil consumption isn't going to decrease, so in about two decades — maybe more but probably less, at the rate we're going — we're going to run out, and if we don't find a way to get at the petroleum buried deep beneath the seas — without destroying the environment — or start converting to nuclear or hydro or solar power, everyone will be plunged back into the dark ages, and people worldwide will starve and/or freeze to death.

>

FtLouie: So, in other words . . . in about ten to fifteen years we're all going to die?

>

SkinnerBx: Basically. How about you? What did YOU learn today?

Um, that you are going to dump me if I don't put out.

But of course I couldn't SAY that. So I just told Michael about how this weekend my mom and Mr G are making an emergency trip to Indiana to introduce Rocky to his Hoosier grandparents. And how Lilly has stabbed me in the back ONCE AGAIN, this time by nominating me as Student Council President, but how she'd said not to worry about it since she 'has a plan'; also about how I hate Geometry already.

```
SkinnerBx: Wait . . . your parents are going
           to Indiana this weekend?
>
FtLouie:   Not my parents. My mom and Mr G.
```

I love Mr G and all, I guess, but it still weirds me out when anyone refers to him as my parent or my dad. I already have a dad.

I forgive Michael for this common mistake, however, as he does not know – as I do – what it's like to come from a broken home.

```
FtLouie:   What do you think your sister could
           be up to anyway? I mean, I would be
           the worst Student Council President
           EVER.
>
SkinnerBx: What day are they leaving?
```

Why is Michael fixated on the fact that Mom and Mr G are going out of town? This is totally the LEAST of my problems.

```
FtLouie:   I don't know. Friday, I guess.
```

Which reminded me:

```
FtLouie:   Do you still want me to come over
```

```
                on Saturday to meet Doo Pak?
>
SkinnerBx: Sure. Or if you want I could come
           over there.
>
FtLouie:   With Doo Pak?
>
SkinnerBx: No. I meant by myself.
>
FtLouie:   Well, if you want to. But I don't
           know why you would. Nobody's going
           to be here but me.
```

Oh no. Rocky's crying again.

I'm not a baby-licker. I'm NOT.

```
SkinnerBx: Mia? Are you still there?
```

But how can they just sit there and listen to him cry like that? It's just WRONG.

```
SkinnerBx: Mia?
>
FtLouie:   Sorry, Michael, I gotta go. I'll
           talk to you later.
```

I wonder if there's a Baby-lickers Anonymous I could join.

Wednesday, September 2, Homeroom

Well, Lana certainly didn't waste any time launching her campaign for Student Council President into over-drive.

When Lilly and I walked into school this morning, it was to find the hallways WALLPAPERED with giant full-colour glossy posters of Lana with the words *VOTE LANA* written underneath them.

Some of the posters are like just headshots, showing Lana tossing her long, shimmery gold hair back and laughing; or with her chin cupped in her hands, smiling with the angelic sweetness of Britney on her first album's cover. In the pictures, Lana doesn't look at all like someone who might grab the back of another girl's bra and hiss, 'Why do you bother to wear one of these when you have nothing to put in it?'

Or someone who might tell a girl in the jet line that college boys expect their girlfriends to Do It.

Some of the other posters show Lana in full-on action shots, like jumping into the air and doing the splits in her cheerleading uniform. One of them shows Lana in her prom dress from last year, standing at the bottom of some staircase. I don't know where, since there was no staircase like it at the actual prom. Maybe her apart-ment? I wouldn't know, of course, having never been invited there.

Lilly took one look at all the posters and then down at her own posters – yes, Lilly spent all last night, while I was learning about Wendell Jenkins, making cam-paign posters for me – and said a very bad word.

Because even though Lilly's posters are very nice – they say *Mia Rules* and *Pick The Princess* – they are only glitter poured over Elmer's glue on white foamcore (for rigidity). Lilly didn't exactly blow up any full-colour glossy headshots of me and plaster the school with them.

'Don't worry, Lilly,' I told her very sympathetically. 'I don't want to be President anyway, so maybe this is for the best.'

Even Boris noticed how sad Lilly was and felt badly for her, which I thought was really nice of him, given how she'd ripped his heart out of his chest and stomped all over it just last May.

'Your posters are much nicer than Lana's,' he told her. 'Because they come from the heart and not some photocopy shop.'

But Lilly ripped her posters in half and stuffed them into a trash can outside the administrative offices anyway. There was glitter *everywhere* by the time she was done.

She did say, kind of darkly, 'She wants war? She's got one.'

But Lilly may have been referring to the fact that they are serving brandade for lunch today in the caf. With cod, the main ingredient in brandade, being nearly extinct due to overfishing, Lilly's been conducting a very vocal campaign on her public-access show against its use in New York City restaurants.

I really wish those producers who optioned Lilly's show would hurry up and find a studio to buy it already. Lilly really needs a new project. She has WAY too much time on her hands.

I have not heard from Michael since I signed off last night. I'm hoping this means he is busy with the whole petroleum-running-out thing and not, you know, that he's breaking up with me because he's realized I'm not exactly the Do It type.

Wednesday, September 2, PE

There should be a law against dodge ball.

Also, what did I ever do to HER? I mean, she's clearly winning this stupid election.

What is the point of even HAVING a bodyguard if he is going to allow me to be pelted in the thigh with red rubber balls?

I definitely think that's going to leave a mark.

Wednesday, September 2, Geometry

'a if b' and 'a only if b'

The phrase 'if and only if' is represented by the abbreviations 'if' and by the symbol <->

a <-> b means both a Æ b and b Æ a.

Is the converse of a true statement necessarily true?

Excuse me, but

WHAT???????????????

There is a Euler diagram appearing on my thigh where Lana hit me with that ball.

Wednesday, September 2, English

Don't you LOVE that pink sweater thing Ms M's wearing! She looks so totally Elle Woods in it! If Elle Woods had black hair, I mean. T.

Yes. It's nice.

R U OK? R U mad about what Lilly did? I think you'd make a really good Student Council Prez, 4 what it's worth.

Thanks, Tina. Actually, I'd sort of forgotten about that. So much other stuff is happening.

What other stuff? That thing with the snails?

You KNOW about that????

It was on the news last night. I guess those people in Monaco are kind of mad.

They have no right to be mad! It's all their fault!

Yeah, the reporter kind of mentioned that. Is that what's bothering U?

No. Well, partly. I mean – can you keep a secret?

Of course!

I know, but like a REAL secret. You CANNOT tell Lilly.

Pinky swear.

OR BORIS!!!!!!!!!!!!!!!!!!!!

PINKY SWEAR!!! I SAID PINKY SWEAR!!!!

OK. Well. It's just that yesterday in the jet line Lana told me that college boys expect their girlfriends to Do It, and that means Michael must be expecting ME to Do It, only I'm not sure I want to. I mean, I guess I WANT to, but not if it involves taking off my clothes in front of him. But I'm not sure there's any way around that. Also I thought college boys only Did It with college girls. But I'm not a college girl, I'm a high-school girl. But then I talked to my mom about it and she said she Did It when she was fifteen with this guy named Wendell Jenkins, but then he married this corn princess named April and my mom hasn't even seen him since. And what if that happens with me and Michael? Like what if we Do It and then we break up because it turns out we want different things and he marries a corn princess? I think that might kill me. Although my mom says she hasn't thought about Wendell in years. I don't know. What should I do?

Just because things didn't work out with Wendell and your mom is no reason to think that you and Michael are also going to break up. And what kind of name is WENDELL anyway?

So you're saying . . . I should Do It?????

76

I don't think Lana really knows what college boys do. She doesn't know any college boys. Or if she does they're probably frat boys. And Michael isn't even in a frat. Besides, Michael really loves you. It's obvious just in the way he looks at you. If you don't want to Do It, don't Do It.

Yeah, but what about what Lana said?????

Michael isn't one of those guys who would dump you just for not Doing It with him. I mean, maybe the guys LANA knows would do this. Like Josh Richter for instance. Or that Ramon guy. He looks kind of sketchy. But not Michael. Because he actually CARES about you. Besides, I really don't think Michael expects you to Do It. At least, not right now.

REALLY??????

Really. I mean, it would be kind of presumptuous of him. You guys have not even been going out for a year. I don't think anyone should Do It with a guy unless they've been going out for at least a year. And then they have to Do It for the first time on prom night. Because when you Do It for the first time, the boy should be wearing a tux. It's only polite.

Tina, I barely managed to get Michael to take me to the prom once. I highly doubt I'm ever going to be able to get him to go again.

Hmm. Well, coronations count. I'm sure it would be just as romantic to Do It for the first time after your coronation.

I'm not having a coronation until after my dad dies and leaves me the throne!!!! I could be as old as Prince Charles by the time that happens!!!!!!!!!!!!!!! I do WANT to Do It before I'm ANCIENT, you know. Just not, you know, NOW.

Well, then you need to tell Michael that. You two really need to have The Talk. You need to get this all out in the open. Because communication is the key to success in a romantic relationship.

Have you and Boris had it? You know, The Talk. About DOING IT?

Of course!!!! I mean, providing things don't work out between Prince William and me, Boris knows that if he ever hopes to be bestowed the gift of my flower, he will need to do it after the prom
- on a king-sized bed with white satin sheets
- in a deluxe suite with Central Park views
- at the Four Seasons over on East Fifty-Second Street
- with champagne and chocolate-covered strawberries upon arrival
- an aromatherapy bath for after
- then waffles for two in bed the next morning

78

Oh. Tina, I don't know how to break this to you . . . but that sounds like a little more than Boris might be able to afford. I mean, he IS still in high school.

I know. That's why I suggested he start saving his allowance now. Also that he better have more than just that one condom he's been carrying around in his wallet for the past two years.

Boris has a condom in his wallet????
Right NOW??????????

Oh yes. He is very proactive. That is one of the reasons I love him.

WOULD YOU GUYS PLEASE QUIT PASSING NOTES AND PAY ATTENTION? THIS IS THE BEST TEACHER WE HAVE EVER HAD AND YOU TWO ARE TOTALLY EMBARRASSING ME WITH YOUR INABILITY TO PAY ATTENTION—
Wait. What's this about a condom?

Nothing! Eyes front!

Who are you guys talking about anyway?

No one, Lilly. Never mind. Look, she's passing back our expository writing samples.

I suppose you think that's going to distract me. I want to know who you guys are talking about. WHO carries around a condom??

Pay attention, Lilly!

Right! Talk about the pot calling the kettle black.
What did you get anyway? An A as usual, Miss I-Always-Get-an-A-in-English?

Well, I DID work really hard on it—

Ha! THAT's not an A!!!! Told you. You really should be paying attention in this class if you're serious about this writing thing.

Wednesday, September 2, French

I don't understand this. I DO NOT UNDERSTAND THIS.

I am a talented writer. I KNOW I am. I have been TOLD I am. By more than one person.

I mean, I'm not saying I don't have more to learn. I know I do. I know I'm no Danielle Steel. Yet. I know I have a lot of work to do before I can ever hope to win a Booker Prize or one of those other awards writers get.

But a B????

I have never got a B for an English assignment in my life!!!!

There must be some mistake.

I was in so much shock after I got my paper back that I think I just sat there with my mouth hanging open for a very long period of time . . . long enough for the line of people gathered around Ms Martinez's desk to thin out enough for her to finally notice me and go, 'Yes, Mia? Do you have a question?'

'This is a B,' was all I managed to choke out. On account of my throat had kind of closed up. And my palms were sweaty. And my fingers were shaking.

Because I have never got a B for an English assignment before. Never, never, never, never . . .

'Mia, you're a very good writer,' Ms Martinez said. 'But you lack discipline.'

'I do?' I licked my lips. They had got all parched, just while I was sitting there, it seemed to me.

Ms Martinez shook her head all sadly.

'I realize it isn't entirely your fault,' Ms Martinez went on. 'You've probably been getting As in your English classes for years using the same cartoonish slapstick

81

humour and slick popular-culture references you used in your writing sample. I'm sure your teachers were too busy dealing with students who couldn't write at all to deal with one who clearly can. But, Mia, don't you see? This kind of self-conscious pseudo-zaniness has no place in a serious expositional work. If you don't learn to discipline yourself, you'll never grow as a writer. Pieces like this one you handed in to me only prove that you have a way with words, NOT that you are a writer.'

I had no idea what she was talking about. All I knew was, I had got a B. A B!!! IN ENGLISH.

'If I write a new one,' I asked, 'will you accept it in the place of this one and cancel out my B?'

'If it's good enough,' Ms Martinez said. 'I don't want you just dashing off something completely over the top again, Mia. I want you to put some thought into it. I want you to make me think.'

'But,' I protested weakly, 'that's what I tried to do in my piece about the snails—'

'By comparing your pouring 10,000 snails into the Bay of Genovia with Pink's refusal to perform for Prince William because he hunts?' Ms Martinez shuddered. 'No, Mia. That didn't make me think. It just made me sad for your generation.'

Thankfully, just then the warning bell went off, so I had to go.

Which is a good thing, because I was just about to throw up all over my desk anyway.

Wednesday, September 2, Gifted and Talented

Michael called during lunch. AEHS students are not supposed to make or receive cellphone calls during class, but at lunch it's OK.

Anyway, he was all, 'What happened to you last night? We were IM-ing, and then you just disappeared!'

Me: 'Oh, yeah. Sorry. Rocky woke up, crying, and I had go sing him back to sleep.'

Michael: 'Oh. So everything's OK?'

Me: 'Well, I mean, if you think the fact that two days into the school year I'm already flunking Geometry, I'm being forced to run for Student Council President against my will, and my new English teacher thinks I'm a talentless hack is OK, then yeah, I guess so.'

Michael: 'I don't think any of those things are OK. Have you talked to – who do you have? Harding? He's a decent guy – about getting some extra help in his class? Or if you want, we can go over the chapter together on Saturday, when I see you. And how could your English teacher think you're a talentless hack? You're the best writer I know. And as for the Student Council thing, Mia, just tell Lilly you don't care WHAT her plan is, you have enough to worry about and you don't want to run. What's the worst that could happen?'

Ha. That is all so easy for Michael to say. I mean, he is not afraid of his sister – not even a little bit, like I am.

83

And Mr Harding? A decent guy? My God, he threw a piece of chalk at Trisha Hayes's head today! Granted, I'd do the same if I thought I could get away with it. But still.

And how does Michael even know what kind of a writer I am? Except for a couple of articles in the school paper last year, and my letters, emails and Instant Messages to him, he has never read anything I've written. I certainly haven't given him any of my poems to read. Because what if he doesn't like them? My writer's spirit would be crushed.

Even more crushed than it is right now.

Me: 'I guess. How's YOUR day going?'

Michael: 'Great. Today in my Principles of Geomorphology we talked about how the ice cap has shrunk by two hundred and fifty million acres – that's the size of California and Texas put together – in the past twenty years, and how if it continues to erode at the rate it's going – about nine per cent per decade – it could vanish altogether by the end of this century, which will, of course, have devastating consequences for life on earth as we know it. Whole species will vanish, and anyone who owns seafront property is essentially going to own underwater property. Unless, of course, we do something to control pollutant emissions that are destroying the ozone layer and allowing this melt-off.'

Me: 'So essentially it doesn't even matter what kind of grade I end up getting in Geometry, since we're all going to die anyway?'

Michael: 'Well, not us necessarily. But our grandkids, for sure.'

Except I was pretty sure Michael didn't mean OUR grandkids, as in the children of kids he and I might have if, you know, we Did It. I believe he was referring to grandkids in the general sense. Such as grandkids he might have with a corn princess he marries later, after he and I have grown apart and gone our separate ways.

Me: 'But I thought we were all going to die in ten years anyway when easily accessible petroleum runs out.'

Michael: 'Oh, don't worry about that. Doo Pak and I have decided to come up with a prototype for a hydrogen-powered car. Hopefully that ought to do the trick. If, you know, the auto industry doesn't try to have us killed for it.'

Me: 'Oh. OK.'

It's nice to know that smart people like Michael are working on this whole petroleum-running-out thing. That leaves the more easily handled problems like, you know, killer algae and Student Council governance to people like me.

Michael: 'So are we all set for Saturday?'

Me: 'You mean my coming over to meet Doo Pak? I think so.'

Michael: 'Actually, what I meant was—'

This is when Lilly tried to wrestle the phone from me.

Lilly:	'Is that my brother? Let me talk to him.'
Me:	'Lilly! Let go!'
Lilly:	'Seriously. I need to talk to him. Mom changed her password again and I can't get into her email.'
Me:	'You shouldn't be reading your mother's email anyway!'
Lilly:	'But how am I going to know what she's telling people about me?'

Here is where I finally managed to wrench the phone out of her hands.

Me:	'Uh, Michael. I'm going to have call you back. After school. OK?'
Michael:	'Oh. OK. Hang in there. Everything's going to be fine.'
Me:	'Yeah. Right.'

It's easy for HIM to say everything's going to be all right. Everything IS going to be all right. For HIM. HE no longer has to be incarcerated in this hellhole for eight hours a day. He gets to take fun classes about how the polar ice cap is going to melt and we're all going to die, while I get to walk down the hall with twenty million posters of Lana Weinberger beaming down at me, going, *Loser! Loser! Princess of what? Oh yeah! Loserville!*

As we left the cafeteria to go put on lipgloss before our next class, I saw Ramon Riveras, the handsome new exchange student, demonstrating Brazilian ball-handling techniques to Lana and some fellow members of the AEHS soccer team, all of whom were paying rapt attention (good thing too, since last year they didn't win one single game). Only instead of a ball Ramon was using an orange, batting it back and forth between his feet. He was saying something too, but I couldn't understand a word, whatever it was. The other members of his team looked confused.

I saw Lana nodding like she understood though. She probably did too. Lana is very familiar with all things Brazilian. I know because I've seen her naked in the shower.

Wednesday, September 2, still Gifted and Talented

Mia. Let's make a list.

No! Lilly, leave me alone! I have too many problems right now to make a list.

What problems? You don't have any problems. You're a princess. You're not flunking Algebra. You have a boyfriend.

That's just it! I have a boyfriend, but apparently he expects me to—

To what?

Never mind. Let's make a list.

Lilly and Mia Rate the Reality Shows

Survivor

Lilly: *A sickening attempt by the media to draw viewers by pandering to the lowest common denominator and appealing to the public's enjoyment of watching others being exploited and humiliated. 0/10*

Mia: Yeah. And who wants to watch people eat bugs? Ew!!!! 0/10

Fear Factor

Lilly: *Ditto. 0/10*

Mia: More bugs. Yuck. 0/10

American Idol

Lilly: *This show is entertaining — if your idea of being entertained is watching young people being ridiculed for attempting to share their talents with the world. 5/10*

Mia: Having had my own dreams crushed all too recently, I am not a fan of watching other people get theirs stomped on. 2/10

Newlyweds: Nick and Jessica

Lilly: *If watching the pathetic ramblings of an uneducated chanteuse who doesn't know the difference between chicken and tuna is your idea of a good time, please feel free to watch this show. I won't try to stop you. 0/10*

Mia: Jessica is not dumb, just inexperienced! She's FUNNY. Also, Nick is hot. Best show EVA! 10/10

Rich Girls

Lilly: *Is anyone really interested in the musings of two young heiresses with nothing more on their minds than cargo pants and boys? 0/10*

Mia: Lilly is wrong about this one too! This is one of the best shows of all time. The Rich Girls care about a lot more than just cargo pants. They want to help people who are too poor to afford cargo pants! 10/10

The Bachelor/ette

Lilly: *Who cares about two stupid people getting together? All they'll end up doing is having kids, and then there'll be more stupid*

*people on this planet. And we're encouraging them by watching
this show! Disgraceful. 0/10*

Mia: Harsh! They're looking for love! What could be
        wrong with that? 5/10

Trading Spaces

Lilly: *I would so never let Hildy near my room. 10/10*

Mia: Have to agree. What is wrong with her? But it
        would be cool to turn her loose on LANA's
        room.10/10

The Real World

Lilly: *Perfection — if your idea of perfection happens to be watching
young people cavort in hot tubs without parental supervision or
any apparent morality. Which mine is. 10/10*

Mia: Why do they all have to be so mean to each
        other? Still, it IS kinda good. 9/10

Queer Eye for the Straight Guy

Lilly: *Five homosexuals give makeovers to hetero men who can't keep
their rooms tidy and don't know any better than to wear acid-
washed jeans. Some proponents of equal rights for the
same-sex oriented fear this show will set their movement back
decades. And yet . . . why WAS that guy wearing that hideous
hairpiece for so long???? 10/10*

Mia: Yeah, and I happen to know someone who could
        still use a little help from the Fab Five, whom
        I'm sure frown on sweater-tucking in. 10/10

***The Simple Life* with Paris Hilton and Nicole Richie**

Lilly: *You're joking, right? I'm supposed to be entertained by an anorexic hotel heiress and Lionel Richie's cokehead kid as they rudely mock the people who were kind enough to take them in? I don't think so. 0/10*

Mia: Um. I kind of have to agree here. Those girls need some MAJOR princess lessons. Maybe next time the Hilton sisters and little Nicole could spend a week with Grandmere! I bet SHE'D have something to say about their piercings. Now that's a reality show I'd LOVE to see!!!!!!! 0/10

Wednesday, September 2, US Government

THEORIES OF GOVERNMENT (cont.)
SOCIAL-CONTRACT THEORY:
Thomas Hobbes, seventeenth-century English philosopher, wrote *Leviathan*, stating that:

Humans originally existed in a 'state of nature'.
  In other words, ANARCHY.

(But anarchy is bad! With anarchy, people can just do whatever they want! With anarchy, for instance, a certain cheerleader who shall remain nameless could wear a pair of shorts that clearly belongs to a member of the men's soccer team under the skirt of her school uniform and make sure everyone notices that she's wearing them by crossing and uncrossing her legs in a very athletic and flamboyant way during her US Government class, as she might be doing RIGHT NOW in flagrant defiance of school regulations. And a certain other person who shall remain nameless might feel like telling on her, but will ultimately decide not to, because tattling is wrong unless someone's life is at stake.)

Hobbes maintained that the original contract between people and state was final, resulting in state's absolutism.
  Fortunately John Locke modified this theory to say that the contract could be renegotiated.

GO, JOHN LOCKE!
GO, JOHN LOCKE!
GO, GO,
GO, JOHN LOCKE!

Wednesday, September 2, Earth Science

Kenny just leaned over to remind me that he has a new girlfriend, Heather, whom he met at Science Camp this summer. Apparently Heather is superior to me in every way (straight As, does gymnastics, doesn't employ slapstick humour or popular-culture references in her expositional essays, isn't a princess, etc.), so despite what I might think, Kenny is completely over me and I can go around flashing my big baby-blue eyes at him all I want, it won't make any difference, he is NOT going to do my Earth Science homework for me this semester.

Whatever, Kenny. First of all, get your prescription checked: my eyes are grey not blue. Second of all, I never asked you to do my Bio homework for me last year. You just started doing it on your own. I'll admit it was wrong of me to LET you, seeing as how I knew I didn't exactly like you in the same way you liked me. But rest assured that's not going to happen again. Because I'm fully going to pay attention in class and do my OWN work. I won't even NEED your help.

And I sincerely hope you and Heather will be happy together. Your children will probably be very, very smart. In the event that you two end up Doing It, I mean. And forget to use birth control. Although that is highly unlikely in the case of two science whizzes.

Kenny is so weird.

No, you know what? *Boys* are weird. Seriously. Maybe that's what I should write my make-up paper on for Ms Martinez. Boys and how weird they are.

For instance, my current top-five favourite movies include:

Dirty Dancing
Flashdance
Bring It On
The original *Star Wars*
Honey

All of which have a similar theme – girl must use her newly acquired talents (dancing) to save herself/relationship/team (well, OK, this is not the plot of *Star Wars* so much. Well, it is, but you have to substitute the word girl with boy. And dancing with the Force).

So you can see why I like them so much.

But Michael's top-five movies – not including the original *Star Wars*, of course – are totally different from mine. There is no single underlying theme to them at all! They're all over the place, theme-wise! And most of them, I don't even know WHY he likes them. There is not even any dancing in them.

Here is a glimpse into the Weird World of Boys and the Movies They Like:

Top-Five Movies Michael Likes (none of which I have seen or ever will):

The Godfather
Scarface
The Texas Chainsaw Massacre
Alien, Aliens, Alien Resurrection, etc.
The Exorcist

Top-Five Movies Michael Likes that I HAVE seen (not including the original *Star Wars*, of course):

Office Space
The Substitute
The Fifth Element
Starship Troopers
SuperTroopers

I would just like to point out that none of the above movies has dancing in it. Not one. In fact, there is no common underlying theme in any of them, with the possible exception of the fact that the guys in them all have super-cute girlfriends.

Basically, men and women have entirely different expectations in their movie-viewing fare. Really, given all that, it is a wonder any of them get together to Do It at all.

On second thoughts, this is probably not a topic Ms Martinez would care to read about. Although *I* find it educational, I doubt *she* will.

She probably never goes to the movies, because they are so pop-culturey. She probably only goes to *films*, like the ones they show at the Angelika. I bet she doesn't even own a TV.

My God. No *wonder* she's the way she is.

PE:	N/A
Geometry:	Exercises pages 20–22
English:	Don't know, was too flipped out to write it down
French:	*Ecrivez une histoire*
	Also, figure out if Perin boy or girl!!!!!!
Gifted and Talented:	N/A
US Government:	What is basis of government acc. to social-contract theory
Earth Science:	Ask Kenny

Wednesday, September 2, limo on the way home from the Plaza

Today when I got to Grandmere's for my princess lesson she announced that we were taking a field trip.

I told her I really don't even have time for a princess lesson today – that my English grade was at stake and that I needed to get home and write a new paper right away.

But Grandmere was completely unimpressed – even when I told her that my future career as an authoress was riding on it. She said royals shouldn't write books anyway – that people only want to read books ABOUT royals, not BY them.

Grandmere so doesn't get it sometimes.

I thought for sure our field trip was going to see Paolo – my roots are totally starting to show – but instead Grandmere took me downstairs to one of the Plaza's many conference rooms. About 200 chairs had been set up in this long room with just a podium in the front with a microphone and a pitcher of water on it.

Only the front row of chairs had people in them. And the people in them were Grandmere's maid, her chauffeur and various members of the Plaza Hotel staff in their green-and-gold uniforms, looking very uncomfortable. Especially Grandmere's maid, who was holding a trembling Rommel on her lap.

At first I thought I'd been set up and that it was a press conference for the snails or something. Except where were the reporters?

But Grandmere said no, it wasn't a press conference. It was to practise.

For the debate.

For Student Council President.

'Uh, Grandmere,' I said. 'There is no debate for Student Council President. Everybody just votes. On Monday.'

But Grandmere way didn't believe me. She went, exhaling a long stream of cigarette smoke, even though there is a Smoking-in-Your-Room-Only policy at the Plaza, 'Your little friend Lilly told me there's a debate.'

'You talked to LILLY?' I could hardly believe it. Lilly and Grandmere HATE each other. With good reason, after the whole Jangbu Pinasa incident.

And now Grandmere is telling me that she and my best friend are in CAHOOTS?

'WHEN DID LILLY TELL YOU THIS?' I demanded, since I didn't believe a word of it.

'Earlier,' Grandmere said. 'Just stand behind the podium and see how it feels.'

'I KNOW how standing behind a podium feels, Grandmere,' I said. 'I've stood behind podiums before, remember? When I addressed the Genovian Parliament on the parking-meter issue.'

'Yes,' Grandmere said. 'But that was before an audience of old men. Here I want you to pretend to be addressing an audience of your peers. Picture them sitting before you, in their ridiculous baggy jeans and backward baseball caps.'

'We wear uniforms to school, Grandmere,' I reminded her.

'Yes, well, you know what I mean. Picture them all sitting there, dreaming of getting their own television show, like that horrible Ashton Kutcher. Then tell me how you would answer this question: What improvements would you implement to help make Albert

Einstein High School a better learning facility, and why?'

Seriously, I don't get her sometimes. It's like she was dropped at birth. Only on to parquet, not on to a futon couch, like I dropped Rocky not too long ago. Except that that totally wasn't my fault on account of Michael walking in unexpectedly wearing a new pair of jeans.

'Grandmere,' I said. 'What is the point of this? THERE IS NO DEBATE.'

'JUST ANSWER THE QUESTION.'

God. She is impossible sometimes.

OK, all the time.

So just to placate her I went behind the stupid podium and said into the microphone, 'Improvements I would implement to help make Albert Einstein High School a better learning facility would include incorporating more meatless entrées into the lunch service for vegan and vegetarian students and, uh, posting homework assignments on the school website every night, so that students who might, er, have forgotten to write them down would know exactly what they have due the next day.'

'Don't hunch so over the podium, Amelia,' Grandmere said critically from where she was standing, blowing her smoke into a large potted rhododendron (Grandmere is so lucky. Because in ten years, when all the petroleum runs out and the polar ice cap is completely melted, she'll probably be dead already from lung cancer on account of all the cigarettes she smokes).

'Stand up straight. Shoulders back. That's it. You may proceed.'

I had totally forgotten what I was talking about.

'What about teachers?' called Grandmere's chauffeur, trying to sound like a baggy-panted Ashton Kutcher wannabe. 'Whadduya gonna do about them, huh?'

'Oh, yeah,' I said. 'Teachers. Isn't it their job to encourage us in our dreams? But I've noticed that certain teachers seem to feel that part of their job description includes crushing our spirit and . . . and . . . stifling our creative impulses! Just because they might, you know, be more entertaining than educational. Are those really the kind of people we want moulding our young minds? Are they?'

'No,' cried one of the maids.

'Damn straight,' yelled Grandmere's chauffeur.

'Oh,' I said, feeling more confident on account of their positive feedback. 'And the, er, video-surveillance cameras outside. I can see how, as a security measure, they are very worthwhile. But if they are being used as—'

'Amelia!' Grandmere screamed. 'Elbows off the podium!'

I took my elbows off the podium.

'—as a tool with which to monitor student behaviour, I have to say, should the administration have the right to essentially spy on us?' I was kind of getting into this debate thing. 'What happens to the tapes in the video cameras after they're full? Are they rewound and taped over or are they stored in some fashion so that the contents might be used against us at some future date? For instance, if one of us gets appointed to the Supreme Court, could a tape of our spraying Joe the Lion in Silly String be made available to reporters and used to bring us down?'

'Feet on the floor, Amelia!' Grandmere shrieked, just because I'd rested one foot on the little shelf in the podium where you're supposed to put your purse or whatever.

'And what about the issue of girls who wear their boyfriends' team athletic shorts beneath their skirts?' I went on. I have to admit, I was kind of enjoying myself. The Plaza maids were totally paying attention to me. One of them even clapped when I said the thing about the security video possibly being used against us if we ran for Supreme Court. 'As sexist as I find the practice, is it the administration's business what goes on beneath the skirts of its female-student population? I say no! No! Don't you dare mess with MY underwear!'

Whoa! This last part brought a standing O from the maids! They were on their feet, cheering for me, like I was . . . I don't know . . . J-Lo or somebody!

I had no idea I was such a brilliant orator. Really. I mean, the parking-meter thing had been nothing compared to this.

But Grandmere wasn't as impressed as everyone else.

'Amelia,' Grandmere said, exhaling a plume of blue smoke. 'Princesses do not beat on the podium with their fists when they make a point.'

'Sorry, Grandmere,' I said.

But I didn't really feel sorry. To tell the truth, I felt kind of stoked. I had no idea how much fun it was to address a roomful of hotel maids. When I'd addressed the Genovian Parliament on the parking-meter issue, hardly any of them had paid attention to me.

But tonight at the hotel, I had those women in the palm of my hand. Really.

Although it would probably be totally different if I really were addressing an audience of people my own age. Like if I really were standing in front of Lana and Trisha and the rest of them, that might be a little different.

Like I actually might throw up on myself.

But I'm not going to worry about it, because it's not like that's ever going to happen. I mean, that I'm actually going to be expected to debate with Lana. Because no one said anything about a debate.

And even if there is one, I'm not going to end up having to do it anyway.

Because Lilly said so. She has a plan.

Whatever that means.

Wednesday, September 2, the Loft

I walked in on utter chaos at 1111 Thompson Street again. Since Mom and Mr G are going to Indiana this weekend, Mom had to move Ladies' Poker Night from Saturday to tonight. So all of the feminist artists from Mom's poker group were sitting around the kitchen table eating moo goo gai pan when I walked in.

They were being really loud too. So loud that when I called Fat Louie he didn't come. I shook his bag of low-fat Iams and everything. Nothing. I actually thought for a minute that Fat Louie had run away – like he'd got out somehow in all the confusion of the feminists coming in. Because, you know, he hasn't been all that happy about sharing the Loft with a new baby. In fact, we've had to chase him out of Rocky's crib more than a few times, since he seems to think it's a bed we put there just for him, since it IS kind of Fat Louie-sized.

And I'll admit, I DO spend a lot of time with Rocky. Time I used to spend giving Fat Louie his kitty massages and all.

But I'm TRYING to be a good mother – a baby-licker to BOTH my brother AND my cat.

I finally found him hiding under my bed…but just his head, because he's so fat. The rest of him wouldn't fit, so his kitty butt was kind of sticking out in the air.

I didn't blame him for hiding, really. Mom's friends can be scary.

Mr G agrees apparently. He was hiding too, it turned out, in the bedroom he and Mom share, trying to watch a baseball game with Rocky. He looked up all startled when I came in to give Rocky a kiss hello.

'Are they gone yet?' he wanted to know, his eyes looking

kind of wild behind his glasses.

'Um,' I said. 'They haven't even started playing.'

'Damn.' Mr G looked down at his son, who wasn't crying for once. He is usually fine if there is a television on. 'I mean, darn.'

I felt a spurt of sympathy for Mr G. I mean, it is not easy being married to my mom. Aside from the whole crazy-painter thing, there's the fact that she seems to be physically incapable of paying a bill on time or even of FINDING the bill when she finally does remember to pay it. Mr G transferred everything to online banking, but it doesn't help, on account of all the cheques my mom gets sent for her art sales ending up wadded up somewhere weird, like in the bottom of her gas-mask container.

I swear, between my inability to divide fractions and her inability to assume any sort of adult responsibility – aside from attending political rallies and breastfeeding – it's a wonder Mr G doesn't divorce us.

'Can I get you anything?' I asked Mr G. 'Some spare ribs? Shrimps with garlic sauce?'

'No, Mia,' Mr G said, wearing a look of long suffering that I recognized only too well. 'But thanks anyway. We'll be fine.'

I left the menfolk to themselves and went into the kitchen to scrounge some food for myself before sneaking off to my bedroom to do all my homework. Fortunately none of my mom's friends paid any attention to me because they were too busy complaining about how male musical artists like Eminem are responsible for turning a generation of young men into misogynists.

Really, I could not stand idly by and allow that kind of

talk in my own home. Maybe it was the after-effects of my powerful speech-giving experience in the empty conference room at the Plaza, but I put down my plate of moo shu vegetable and told my mom's friends that their argument against Eminem was specious (I don't even know what this word means, but I've heard Michael and Lilly use it a lot) and that if they would just take a moment to listen to 'Cleaning Out My Closet' (one of Rocky's favourites by the way), they would know that the only women Eminem hates are his mom and the hos that be trippin' on him.

This statement, which I felt was quite reasonable, was met by utter silence by the feminist artists. Then my mom went, 'Is that the door? It must be Vern from downstairs. He gets so upset these days when he thinks we're having a party and we haven't invited him. I'll be right back.'

And she scurried to the door even though I hadn't heard the buzzer ring.

Then one of the feminists went, 'So, Mia, is your defence of Eminem the kind of thing your grandmother teaches you during your princess lessons?'

And all the other feminists laughed.

But then I remembered that I actually needed some advice on the feminist front so I was all, 'Hey, you guys, I mean, women, do you know if it's true that all college boys expect their girlfriends to Do It?'

'Uh, not just college boys,' said one of the women while the rest of them laughed uproariously.

So it IS true. I should have known. I mean, I'd kind of been hoping that Lana was just trying to make me feel bad. But now it looks as if she might actually have been telling the truth.

'You look worried, Mia,' commented Kate, the performance artist who likes to stand up on stage and smear chicken fat on herself to make a statement about the beauty industry.

'She's always worried,' said Gretchen, a welder who specializes in metal replicas of body parts. Particularly of the male variety. 'She's Mia, remember?'

All the feminist artists laughed uproariously at that too.

This made me feel bad. Like my mom's been talking about me behind my back. I mean, I talk about HER behind HER back of course. But it's different when your own mother has been talking about YOU.

Clearly Lilly is not the only one who thinks I'm a baby-licker.

'You spend way too much time freaking out about things, Mia.' Becca, the neon-light artist, waved her margarita glass at me knowingly. 'You should stop thinking so much. I don't remember thinking half as much as you do when I was your age.'

'Because you were already on lithium when you were her age,' Kate pointed out.

But Becca ignored her.

'Is it the snails?' Becca wanted to know.

I just blinked at her. 'The what?'

'The snails,' she said. 'You know, the ones you dumped in the bay. Are you worried about how everyone is upset about them?'

'Um,' I said, wondering if she, like Tina, had seen this on the news. 'I guess so.'

'That's understandable,' Becca said. 'I'd be worried too. Why don't you take up yoga?' she suggested. 'That always helps me to relax.'

'Or watch more TV,' suggested Dee, who enjoys creating totem poles and then dancing around them with pieces of liver strapped beneath her arms.

I couldn't believe this. I was being told by these intelligent women to watch MORE TV? Clearly they're not friends with Karen Martinez.

'Stop picking on Mia.' Windstorm, who happens to be one of my mom's oldest friends AND a midwife AND a minister AND a professional choreographer, got up to put more ice in the blender. 'She's got a right to think too much and freak out if she wants to. There isn't anything more stressful than being a fifteen-year-old, with the possible exception of being a fifteen-year-old princess.'

I had never thought of that before. DO I think too much? Do other people not think as much as I do? Except according to Ms Martinez, I don't think ENOUGH . . .

'I guess it must have been one of those delivery boys, slipping a menu under the door,' my mom said, coming back to the table. 'What'd I miss?'

'Nothing,' I said, taking my plate and hurrying off to my room. 'Have fun, you guys! I mean, women!'

I wonder if Windstorm is right. About my thinking too much. Maybe that's my problem. I can't shut my brain off. Maybe other people can, but I can't. I've never actually tried, of course, because who wants to have an empty head? Except for, you know, the Hilton sisters. Because it's probably easier to party all the time if you aren't worrying about killer algae or all the petroleum running out.

Still, maybe there's something to it. I can hardly sleep at night, my mind is so busy whirring away up there, wondering what I'm going to do if aliens come in the night and take over everything or whatever. I would LOVE to be able to shut my mind off the way other people seem to be able to. If Windstorm is right anyway.

Ooooo, Michael's Instant Messaging me now!

SkinnerBx: So are we still getting together on
Saturday?

Right as Michael asked this, I got another Instant Message.

WomynRule: BL, what are you doing Saturday?

Seriously. Why me? WHY?

FtLouie: I can't talk to you right now. I'm
IM-ing your brother.
>
WomynRule: Tell him Mom's turning his room
into a shrine to the Reverend Moon.
>
FtLouie: LILLY! GO AWAY!
>
WomynRule: Just keep Saturday free, OK? It's
important. It has to do with the
campaign.
>
FtLouie: I already have plans with your
brother on Saturday.
>
WomynRule: What, are you two going to Do It
then or something?

FtLouie: NO WE ARE NOT GOING TO DO IT THEN.
            WHO TOLD YOU THAT?
>

WomynRule: No one! Jeez! Don't get the princess
            panties in a royal twist. Why would
            you even get so mad about that
            unless — wait — ARE YOU GUYS DOING
            IT???? AND YOU DIDN'T TELL
            ME??????????
>

FtLouie: NO, FOR THE LAST TIME WE ARE NOT
            DOING IT!!!!
>

SkinnerBx: Doing what? What are you talking
            about?

OH MY GOD.

FtLouie: Not you! I meant to send that to
            Lilly!
>

SkinnerBx: Wait, is Lilly IM-ing you right now
            too?
>

WomynRule: I can't believe you're Doing It with
            my brother. That is so gross. You
            know, he has hair growing out of his
            toes. Like a hobbit.
>

FtLouie: Lilly! SHUT UP!
>

SkinnerBx: Is Lilly giving you a hard time?
            Tell her if she doesn't cut it out

```
                I'll tell Mom about the time she did
                the 'gravitational experiment' with
                Grandma's Hummel figurines.
>

FtLouie:    BOTH  OF  YOU!  STOP  IT!!!!  YOU'RE
            DRIVING  ME  INSANE!!!!
>

FtLouie:    terminated
```

Seriously. I'm GLAD I'm a baby-licker if it means Rocky
and I will never end up like those two.

Thursday, September 3, Homeroom

Oh.
   My.
   God.
   That is all I have to say.

Thursday, September 3, PE

They're even in the gym. I don't know how she did it. But they're even HANGING FROM THE ROPES IN THE GYM.

Seriously.

They're in the showers too. Encased in plastic sheets, so they won't get wet.

I know we learned in Health and Safety that it's physically impossible to die from embarrassment, but I might turn out to be the exception to the rule.

Thursday, September 3, Geometry

THEY ARE EVERYWHERE.

GIANT FULL-COLOUR HEADSHOTS OF ME IN MY TIARA. WITH MY SCEPTRE. From when I got formerly introduced to the people of Genovia last December.

And underneath my photo, it says:

Vote for Mia.

Then underneath that:

PIT.

PIT. What does that even MEAN?????

Everyone is talking about them. EVERYONE. I was just sitting here, innocently going over my homework, when Trisha Hayes came in and was all, 'Nice try, *PIT.* But it won't make any difference. You may be a princess, but Lana is the most popular girl in school. She's going to decimate you on Monday.'

'Somebody's been studying up on their vocab,' is what I said to Trisha. Because of her use of the word decimate.

But that's not what I wanted to say. What I wanted to say was, 'IT WASN'T ME!!!! I DIDN'T DO IT!!!! I DON'T EVEN KNOW WHAT PIT MEANS!!!!!'

But I couldn't. Because everyone was looking at us. Including Mr Harding. Who took five points off Trisha's homework for not being in her seat by the time the bell rang.

'You can't do that,' Trisha had the bad judgement to say to him.

'Uh,' Mr Harding said. 'Excuse me, Miss Hayes, but yes, I can.'

'Not for long,' Trisha said. 'When my friend Lana is Student Council President, she's going to abolish tardy demerits.'

'And what do you have to say about that, Miss Thermopolis?' Mr Harding wanted to know. 'Is abolishing tardy demerits part of your campaign strategy as well?'

'Um,' I said. 'No.'

'Really?' Mr Harding looked way interested. Except that I think he was only interested because he found the whole thing vaguely hilarious. On some weird teacher level. 'And why is that?'

'Um,' I said, feeling my ears starting to turn red. That's because I could tell that everyone in the entire class was staring at us. 'Because I thought I might concentrate on stuff that actually matters. Like the lack of choice in vegetarian entrées in the cafeteria. And the cameras they've installed outside by Joe, which are a violation of our right to privacy. And the fact that some of the teachers around here don't grade objectively.'

And to my VERY great surprise, some of the people at the back of the room started to clap. Really. Like that slow clap they do in the movies, the kind where everybody eventually joins in, until it turns into fast clapping.

Only Mr Harding nipped it in the bud before it ever turned to fast clapping by going, 'All right, all right, that's enough of that. Turn to page fourteen and let's get started.'

Oh my God. This presidential thing has got WAY out of hand.

Syllogism = argument of the form a Æ b (first premise)

b Æ c (second premise)

Therefore: a Æ c (conclusion)

WHATEVER. Why did they have to use the one of me with my SCEPTRE??? I look like a total freak in that one.

Note to self: look up *decimate*.

Thursday, September 3, English

LILLY!!! WHERE DID YOU GET THOSE POSTERS????

Where do you think I got them? And stop yelling at me!

I'm not yelling. I'm very calmly asking . . . Did you get those posters from my grandmother?

Yes, of course I did. What do you think, I paid for them myself? Do you have any idea how much full-colour posters that size cost? I could have used up the entire annual budget for Lilly Tells It Like It Is *on the copy-setting alone!*

But I thought you hated Grandmere! Why would you do something like that? Like let my grandmother be involved in this?

Because, in case you haven't noticed, this election is important to me, Mia. I REALLY want us to win. We HAVE to win. It's the only way we're going to save this school from becoming a completely fascist state under the tyrannical reign of Gutless Gupta.

But, Lilly, I DON'T WANT TO BE STUDENT COUNCIL PRESIDENT.

Don't worry. You won't be.

THAT MAKES NO SENSE! I mean, Lilly, I know everyone just assumes Lana is going to win because she wins everything, but things are getting really weird. In Geometry today, I said something about those cameras outside being a violation of our rights to privacy, and someone started CLAPPING for me.

It's happening. Just like I KNEW it would!

What's happening?????

Never mind. Just keep doing what you're doing. It's great. It's so NATURAL. I could never be that natural.

BUT I'M NOT DOING ANYTHING!

That's what's so great about it. Now come on, pay attention to this. You need to know this stuff if you're going to be a writer and all.

Lilly, is there going to be a debate? Because Grandmere said something about a debate.

Shhhh. Pay attention. Hey, what's going on with my brother anyway? Are you two really Doing It?

STOP TRYING TO CHANGE THE SUBJECT! IS THERE GOING TO BE A DEBATE?????
LILLY!!!!
LILLY!!!!!!!!!!!!! ANSWER ME!!!!!!

I don't think Lilly's going to answer you. Is there anything I can do?

116

Oh. Hi, Tina. No. Just . . . well, you wouldn't be willing to get your bodyguard to shoot me, would you? Because I'd really appreciate it.

> Um, Wahim's not allowed to shoot anyone unless they're trying to kidnap me. You know that.

I know. But I still wish I were dead.

> I'm so sorry. The election thing?

That and Michael and everything else.

> Did you and Michael have that talk like I told you to?

No. When could we have had a talk? I never get to see him any more because he's always in class, learning new ways we're all going to die. And you can't talk about Doing It – or, in this case, NOT Doing It – over the phone or IM-ing. It's kind of a face-to-face topic.

> That's true. So when are you going to talk about it?

Saturday, I guess. I mean, that's the earliest we're going to see each other.

> Good! Don't you love Ms M in those totally adorable culottes! Who knew culottes could even BE adorable?

117

You know, someone could be wearing culottes and still not be . . . um, right.

What do you mean? Ms Martinez is ALWAYS right. She loves Jane Austen, doesn't she?

Um, yes. But maybe not for the same reasons we do.

You mean not because Colin Firth looks so hot every time he dives into that pond? But what other reason IS there to love Jane Austen?

Never mind. Pretend I didn't say anything.

Do you think Ms M knows how in real life Emma Thompson had the baby of the guy who played Willoughby???? Because even though he played a bad guy in Sense and Sensibility, I'm sure he's really nice in person. And besides, Emma needed to find love after that Kenneth Branagh left her for Helena Bonham Carter.

Sometimes I wish I could live inside Tina's head instead of mine. I swear. It must be very restful there.

Thursday, September 3, ladies' room, Albert Einstein High School

How do I always end up here? Writing in my journal in a stall of the ladies' room, I mean? It is becoming like a ritual or something.

Anyway, it all started innocently enough. We were talking about last night's episode of *The OC* when next thing I knew Tina was going, 'Hey, did you tell Lilly yet?'

And Lilly was all, 'Tell me what?'

And I totally thought Tina meant the thing about Doing It with Michael and I mouthed *PINKY SWEAR* at her until she went, 'About your parents going away to Indiana this weekend, I mean,' which I must have mentioned to her in a moment of weakness, although I don't remember doing so.

Lilly looked at me, all excited. 'They are? That's great! We can have another party!'

Hello. You would think Lilly of ALL people wouldn't want to come to another party at my place. Or at least would be a little more sensitive about the fact that her ex, whom she LOST forever at my last party, was sitting right there.

But she totally didn't seem to notice or care.

'So what time can we come over?' she wanted to know.

'Just because my mom and Mr G are going away does NOT mean I'll be having a party,' I yelled, all panicky.

'Yeah,' Lilly said, looking thoughtful. 'I forgot. You're heir to the throne of Genovia. It's not like they're going to leave you there alone. But that's OK. We can probably get Lars and Wahim to go off by themselves somewhere—'

'NO,' I said, 'that's not it. I'm not having a party because the last time I had one, it was a total disaster, in which SOME people thought it would be a good idea to play Seven Minutes in Heaven, and got CAUGHT at it by my stepfather.'

'Yeah,' Lilly said. 'But this time, Mr Gianini won't be there—'

'NO PARTIES,' I said in my most princessy voice.

Lilly just sniffed and went, 'Just because you got a B on an English paper, don't take it out on me.'

Oh, OK, Lilly, I won't. And just because YOUR parents don't trust you enough to let you stay alone in the house on account of that one time you set off the sprinkler system in the building with your home-made lighter-and-Rave-hairspray flamethrower, don't take it out on me.

Only of course I didn't say that out loud.

'Wait,' Boris said. 'YOU got a B on an English paper, Mia? How is that possible?'

So then I had no choice but to break the news to everyone at the lunch table. You know, about Ms Martinez being a big, huge über-phoney.

They were all shocked of course.

'But she has such cute clogs!' Tina cried, her heart clearly breaking.

'It just goes to show,' Boris said, 'that you can't tell what's in someone's heart by the way he or she dresses.' He shot a very significant look at me while he said this.

But I don't care. Tucking your sweater into your pants is not a good look for ANYONE.

'She probably means well,' Tina said, since she tries to find the good in everyone.

'There is never any justification for crushing the

120

artistic spirit,' Ling Su said – and, since she can draw better than anyone in our whole school, she would know. 'Lots of so-called critics and reviewers *meant* well when they ravaged the works of the Impressionists in the nineteenth century. But if artists like Renoir and Monet had followed their advice, some of the greatest works of art in the world would never have been created.'

'Well, I wouldn't exactly compare my writing to a Renoir painting,' I felt obligated to say. 'But thanks, Ling Su.'

'The thing is, even if Mia's writing DOES stink,' Boris said, in his usual blunt fashion, 'does a teacher really have the right to tell her so?'

'It does sort of seem anti-educational,' Shameeka said.

'Something's got to be done about this,' Ling Su said. 'The question is, what?'

But before we could come up with anything, this dark shadow fell over our lunch table and we looked up and there was . . .

Lana.

Our hearts sank. Well, mine did anyway.

Lana was accompanied by the new Grand Moff Tarkin to her Darth Vader, Trisha Hayes.

'Nice posters, *PIT*,' Lana said. Only of course she was being sarcastic. 'But they aren't going to do you any good.'

'Yeah,' Trisha said. 'We took a random poll of the cafeteria, and if the election were today you'd only get sixteen votes.'

'You mean there are sixteen people in this cafeteria,' Lilly said mildly as she peeled the chocolate coating off a Ho Ho, 'who were willing to tell you to your face that

121

they aren't voting for you? God, I had no idea there were so many masochists in this school.'

'Keep sucking on that Twinkie, fatty,' Lana said. 'And we'll see who's the masochist.'

'It's a Ho Ho,' Boris pointed out, because that is what Boris does.

Lana didn't even look at him.

'And you know what else?' Lana said. 'I'm going to trounce you at Monday's debate during Assembly. Nobody at Albert Einstein wants a snail-dumper as President.'

Snail-dumper! That's almost as bad as being called a baby-licker!

But before I had a chance to defend my snail-dumping ways, Lana had flounced away.

Since I didn't want to humiliate Lilly by screaming at her in front of her ex, especially now that he's hot, I just looked at her and went, 'Lilly. Ladies' room. NOW.'

Somewhat to my surprise she followed me in here.

'Lilly,' I said, summoning all of the people skills Grandmere has taught me. Not, you know, that Grandmere has actually taught me any useful skills for dealing with people. It's just so hard dealing with Grandmere that I have sort of acquired some along the way. 'This has gone on long enough. I never wanted to run for Student Council President in the first place, but you kept telling me you had a plan. Lilly, if you really have a plan, I want to know what it is. Because I am sick of people calling me PIT – whatever that means. And there is NO WAY I'm going to debate Lana on Monday. NO FREAKING WAY.'

'Princess in Training,' was all Lilly had to say to that.

I just looked at her like she's a mental case. Which

I'm pretty sure she is.

'Princess in Training,' she said again. 'That's what PIT stands for. Since you asked.'

'I told you,' I said through gritted teeth, 'not to call me that any more!'

'No,' Lilly said. 'You said not to call you baby-licker or POG – Princess of Genovia. Not PIT – Princess in Training.'

'Lilly.' My teeth were still gritted. 'I do not want to be Student Council President. I have enough problems right now. I do not need this. I do not need to debate Lana Weinberger on Monday in front of the whole school.'

'Do you want to make this school a better place or not?' Lilly wanted to know.

'Yeah,' I said. 'I do. But it's hopeless, Lilly. I can't beat Lana. She's the most popular girl in school. No one is going to vote for me.'

At that moment, even though I'd thought we were alone in the ladies' room, a toilet flushed. The next thing I knew a tiny little freshman girl came out of a stall and over to the sinks to wash her hands.

'Um, excuse me, Your Highness,' she said to me after Lilly and I had stared at her in dumbfounded silence for several seconds. 'But I really admire that thing you did with the snails. And *I'm* planning on voting for you.'

Then she threw her paper towel in the trash and walked out.

'Ha!' said Lilly. 'HA HA! See? I TOLD you! Something's HAPPENING, Mia. It's like a groundswell of resentment towards Lana and her ilk. The people are sick of the reign of the popular crowd. They want a new queen. Or princess, as the case may be.'

'Lilly—'

'Just keep doing what you're doing and everything will be fine.'

'But, Lilly—'

'And keep Saturday during the day open. You can do whatever it is you're doing with my brother at night. Just give me the day.'

'Lilly, I don't WANT to be President,' I screamed.

'Don't worry,' Lilly said, giving my cheek a pat. 'You won't be.'

'But I also don't want to be humiliatingly beaten by Lana in a student election either!'

'Don't worry,' Lilly said, adjusting one of her many barrettes in the mirror above the sinks. 'You won't be.'

'Lilly,' I said. 'HOW CAN BOTH OF THOSE THINGS NOT HAPPEN???? IT'S IMPOSSIBLE!!!!'

But then the bell rang and she left.

I wonder if there's a disorder in Yahoo! Health for whatever it is that's wrong with my best friend.

Thursday, September 3, US Government

THEORIES OF GOVERNMENT (cont.)
THEORY OF FORCE:

Religion and economics play important roles in history. As a result, this theory says:

Governments have always forced the people within their reach to pay tribute or tax.

This became sanctioned by custom and people developed myths and legends to justify their rule.

(Sort of like the way people accept that the jocks and the cheerleaders run this school, despite the fact that they don't necessarily make the best grades, so it's not like they're the smartest group of people here, nor are they even very nice to those of us who don't eat, drink and breathe sports and partying. How are they even QUALIFIED to lead us? And yet their word is Law and everyone pays tribute to them by not calling them on their cruelty to others or by not telling on them when they flagrantly disregard school policy, such as smoking on school grounds and wearing their boyfriends' shorts beneath their skirts. This is just wrong. The misdeeds of a few are having a negative impact on the many, and that's not fair. I wonder what John Locke would have to say about it.)

Thursday, September 3, Earth Science

Why won't Kenny stop talking about his girlfriend? I'm sure she's nice and all, but really, does he HAVE to keep reciting every conversation he's ever had with her to me?

Magnetic field

1. Not constant – varies in strength but hardly detectable

2. Poles wander – number of times poles have reversed

3. Reversal of magnetic field – during times poles reverse, field disappears, allowing ions to hit earth, mutations, climatic ruin, etc.

Last major reversal, 800,000 years ago, magnetic particles that were pointing North about-faced to point South

PE:	N/A
Geometry:	Exercises, pages 33–35
English:	Strunk and White, pages 30–54
French:	*Lire L'Etranger pour Lundi*
Gifted and Talented:	N/A
US Government:	Definite force theory of gov.
Earth Science:	Orbital perturbations

Thursday, September 3, limo on the way home from the Plaza

So when I walked into Grandmere's suite at the Plaza for my princess lesson this afternoon, what did I find?

A pop quiz about seating arrangements for heads of state at a diplomatic banquet? Oh, no.

A waltz I needed to learn for some ball? Huh-uh.

Because those would be the kind of things you'd EXPECT at a princess lesson. And Grandmere likes to keep me on my toes apparently.

Instead, I found about two-dozen journalists gathered in her suite, all eager to discuss my Student Council Presidency campaign with myself and my campaign manager, Lilly.

That's right. Lilly. Lilly was sitting, cool as a cucumber, on a blue velvet settee, with Grandmere, answering the reporters' questions.

When the journalists saw me come in, they all jumped up and shoved microphones in my face instead of Lilly's and went, 'Your Highness, Your Highness! Are you looking forward to your debate on Monday?' And, 'Princess Mia, do you have anything you'd like to say to your constituents?'

I had one thing I wanted to say to one constituent. And that was, 'LILLY! WHAT ARE YOU DOING HERE?'

That was when Grandmere sprang into action. She hurried up and draped an arm around my shoulder and went, 'Your dear friend Lilly and I were just chatting with these nice reporters about your campaign for Student Council President, Amelia. But what they'd really like is a statement from you. Why don't you be a darling and give them one?'

The minute Grandmere calls you *darling*, you know something is up. But, of course, I already knew something was up because Lilly was there. How had she even got to the Plaza so fast? She must have taken the subway while I'd been tied up in traffic in the limo.

'Yes, *Princess*,' Lilly said, reaching out to take my hand, then pulling me – none too gently – down on to the settee beside her. 'Tell the nice reporters about all the reforms you're planning to make at AEHS.'

I leaned over, pretending I was reaching for a watercress sandwich from the tray Grandmere's maid had set out for the reporters, who are always hungry – and not just for a story. But then, as I grabbed one of the dainty little sandwiches, I hissed in Lilly's ear, 'Now you've gone too far.'

But Lilly just smiled blandly at me and said, 'I think the princess would like some tea, Your Highness.'

To which Grandmere replied, 'But of course. Antoine! Tea for the princess!'

The press conference went on for an hour, with reporters from all over the country peppering me with questions about my campaign platform. I was just thinking that it must be a REALLY slow news day if my running for Student Council President qualified as a decent story, when one of the reporters asked me a question that shed a little light on just why Grandmere was so keen on my making an ass of myself in front of Middle America – and not just my fellow AEHS students.

'Princess Mia,' a journalist from the *Indianapolis Star* asked. 'Isn't it true that the only reason you're running for Student Council President – and the only reason we were invited here today – is that your family is trying to distract the news media from the real story currently hitting headlines in Europe: your act of eco-terrorism concerning the dumping of 10,000 snails into the Genovian bay?'

Suddenly, two-dozen microphones were shoved into my face. I blinked a few times then went, 'But that wasn't an act of eco-terrorism. I did that to save the—'

Then Grandmere was clapping her hands and going, 'Who wants a nice glass of grappa? Come now, real Genovian grappa. No one can resist that!'

But none of the reporters was falling for it.

'Princess Mia, would you like to comment on the fact that Genovia is currently being considered for expulsion from the EU, thanks to your selfish act?'

Another one cried, 'How does it feel, Your Highness, to know that you're single-handedly responsible for destroying your own nation's economy?'

'Wh-What?' I couldn't believe it. What were these reporters talking about?

For once, Lilly came to my rescue.

'People!' she cried, leaping to her feet. 'If you don't have any more questions about Mia's campaign for school president, then I'm afraid I'm going to have to ask you to leave!'

'Cover-up!' someone yelled. 'That's all this is! A cover-up to keep us from the real story!'

'Princess Mia, Princess Mia,' someone else called as Lars began herding – or, to put it more accurately, bodily removing – all of the reporters from the suite. 'Are you a member of ELF, the Earth Liberation Front? Do you want to make a statement on behalf of other eco-terrorists like yourself?'

'Well,' Grandmere said, downing half a Sidecar in

one gulp as Lars finally closed the doors on the last of the reporters. 'That went well, don't you think?'

I couldn't believe it. I just sat there in total shock. Eco-terrorism? ELF? All because of some SNAILS????

Lilly picked up her Palm Pilot (when did she get one of those???) and strolled over to where Grandmere was standing.

'Right. So we've got *Time* magazine at six, and *Newsweek* at six-thirty,' Lilly said. 'I heard from NPR and I definitely think we should squeeze them in this evening – drive time, you know. It can't hurt. And we got a request from New York One for Mia to go on tonight's broadcast of *Inside Politics*. I've got them to swear there won't be any questions about the E word. What do you think?'

'Marvellous,' Grandmere said, taking another swig from her Sidecar. 'What about Larry King?'

Lilly tapped the headset she'd slipped on and said, 'Antoine? Have you got hold of Larry K yet? No? Well, get on it.'

Larry K? The E word? What was HAPPENING?

Which is exactly what I wailed.

Grandmere and Lilly looked at me as if only just realizing I was there at all.

'Oh,' Lilly said, taking off the headset. 'Mia. Right. The ELF thing? Don't worry about it. Par for the course.'

PAR FOR THE COURSE???? Since when has Lilly known anything about golf?

'We didn't want to trouble you, Amelia,' Grandmere said coolly as she lit a cigarette. 'It's nothing really. Tell me, is that really how you're wearing your hair these days? Wouldn't you like it better if it were a little . . . shorter?'

130

'What is going on?' I demanded, ignoring her hair question. 'Is Genovia REALLY going to get expelled from the EU for what I did with the snails?'

Grandmere exhaled a long plume of blue smoke.

'Not if I have anything to say about it,' she informed me casually.

My heart seemed to twist inside my chest. It's true!

'Can they do that?' I demanded. 'Can the European Union really kick us out because of a few snails?'

'Of course not.' This came from my dad, who'd wandered into the room, a cellphone clutched to his ear. I felt a momentary relief until I realized he wasn't speaking to me. He was talking into his cellphone.

'No,' he yelled at whoever was on the end of the line, bending to scoop up a handful of leftover sandwiches from the tray before heading back to his own suite. 'She was acting entirely on her own accord, not in the name of any global organization. Oh, really? Well, I'm sorry you feel that way. Maybe when you have a teenage daughter of your own you'll understand.'

He slammed the door on his way out.

'Well,' Grandmere said, stubbing out her cigarette and reaching for the rest of her Sidecar. 'Shall we talk about Amelia's platform then?'

'Excellent idea,' Lilly said and pressed some buttons on her Palm Pilot.

So now at least I know why GRANDMERE is so behind this presidency thing. It's the only thing she can think of to keep reporters distracted from the whole 'Genovia being kicked out of the EU for eco-terrorism' thing.

But what's LILLY's excuse? I mean, she's the LAST person I ever thought Grandmere could turn to the dark side.

Et tu, Lilly?

My dad came back into the room between my *Time* and *Newsweek* interviews. He looked way stressed. I felt really bad and apologized to him about the whole snail-dumping thing.

He seemed to take it in his stride.

'Don't worry too much about it, Mia,' he said. 'We'll probably get through this if I can manage to impress upon everyone the fact that you were acting on your own accord as a private citizen, and not on my behalf.'

'And maybe,' I added hopefully, 'when people see that the snails are only doing good and not anything bad, they'll change their minds.'

'That's just it,' my dad said. 'Your snails aren't doing anything at all. According to the latest reports I've had from the royal Genovian naval scuba squad, they're all just sitting down there. They are not, as you so passionately assured me they would, eating that damned seaweed.'

This was very disheartening to hear.

'Maybe they're still in shock,' I said. 'I mean, they were flown in from South America. They've probably never been that far from home before. It might take a while before they get acclimatized to their new environment.'

'Mia, they've been down there for almost two weeks. In two weeks you'd think they'd get a little hungry and eat something.'

'Yeah, but maybe they had a big meal on the plane,' I said, feeling desperate. 'I mean, I requested that they be kept as comfortable as possible during transport.'

My dad just looked at me.

'Mia,' he said. 'Do me a favour. From now on, if you

come up with any more grand schemes to save the bay from killer algae, run them by me first.'

Ouch.

Poor Dad. It's really hard being a prince.

I left right after that. But Lilly stayed. LILLY STAYED WITH MY GRANDMA. Because she still hadn't managed to get through to Larry. Lilly told me if she could get me on Larry King, I'd be a shoo-in to beat Lana on Monday.

But I disagree. If it were *TRL*, maybe. But no one at AEHS watches CNN. Except Lilly of course.

Anyway. Now I get why Grandmere is so into the idea of my running for Student Council President.

But what's LILLY getting out of it? I mean, you would think, mad as she is about the security-camera thing, SHE'D be the one running for President. What's up with that anyway?

Thursday, September 3, the Loft

So guess where I'm staying while my mom and Mr G are out of town? Yeah. That'd be at the Plaza.

WITH GRANDMERE.

Oh, they're getting me my own room. BELIEVE ME. No WAY am I sleeping in the same suite as Grandmere. Not after that time she stayed over at the Loft. I barely slept a wink the whole time she was there, she snored so loud. I could hear her all the way out in the living room.

Not to mention that she's a total bathroom hog.

I guess I kind of expected it. I mean, no way would Mom and Mr G let me stay alone at the Loft. Even if the entire Genovian national guard was positioned on the roof of our building, ready to take out any potential international princess hostage-takers. Not after what happened during my birthday party.

Not that I even care. Not now that I am responsible for making the country over which I will one day rule the most hated land in Europe. Which is pretty hard to do considering, you know, France.

I didn't actually think it was possible for me to get more stressed than I already was, considering that:

- I think I might be flunking Geometry after only three days of it.
- My best friend is making me run for Student Council President against the most popular girl in school, who is going to crush me like a bug in a humiliating defeat in front of the entire student body on Monday.
- My English teacher – the one I was so excited about and whom I was sure was going to help

134

mould me into the kind of writer I know in my heart I have the potential to be – seems to think my prose is so bad it should never be unleashed upon the unsuspecting public. Well, more or less.

- My boyfriend apparently expects me to Do It.
- I'm a baby-licker.

Thank God to all of that I get to add that I had 10,000 snails flown from South America and dumped into the Genovian bay in the hopes that they would consume the killer algae currently destroying our delicate ecosystem, only to discover that South American snails apparently don't like European food and that Genovia's neighbours now want nothing to do with us. Yay!

Why can't I do ANYTHING right?

Maybe Becca is right. Maybe I *should* take up yoga. Except that I tried it that one time with Lilly and her mom at the Ninety-Second Street Y, and they made you stick your butt up in the air the whole time. How is sticking your butt up into the air supposed to make you feel less stressed? It just made me feel MORE stressed because I kept wondering what everyone was thinking about my butt.

Ordinarily, to soothe my frazzled nerves, I might write a poem or something.

However, it is impossible for me to write poetry, knowing, as I do, that at this very moment Karen Martinez is poring over the piece of my soul that I handed to her. I hope she is aware that she is currently holding all my dreams of ever succeeding as a novelist – or at least a hard-hitting international journalist – in her black-nail-polished fingers. I sincerely hope she won't squash them like a bug under Fat Louie's massive paw.

I know, you know, that it's pretty unlikely I'll ever actually get to DO any writing once I take over the throne, since I'll be too busy begging the EU to let us back into it and all.

But I think I would have liked to see a book or even just a newspaper article with the words 'by Mia Thermopolis' on it.

Now I have to go make sure my mom is up on all the plane's safety regulations. I mean, it is not like they are buying a seat for Rocky. She is going to have to hold him the whole time. I hope, in the event that their plane goes down, she is prepared to use her body as a human shield to keep Rocky from being consumed in a fiery conflagration.

Also that Mr G knows he has to count the number of rows between his seat and the nearest emergency exit so that in the event of a water landing and the plane sinking and the lights going out, he will still be able to lead my mom and Rocky to safety.

Thursday, September 3 later, the Loft

Geesh! Talk about touchy! I don't know why they got so mad. It's important to know plane safety. I mean, that's why the airline companies print those cards they stick in the back of the seats. Hello. Good thing I have been collecting them for years, so I was able to use them as illustrations for my baby-safety talk just now.

You would think people would be a little more appreciative of my proactiveness.

Someone's IM-ing me . . .

Ooooooooooooooooo, it's Michael!

SkinnerBx: Hey! You're home! Saw you on New York One.

\>

FtLouie: You SAW that??? OMG, how embarrassing.

\>

SkinnerBx: No, you were good. Is that really true about the EU though?

\>

FtLouie: Apparently. My dad says it will be all right though. He thinks. He hopes.

\>

SkinnerBx: They should all be ashamed of themselves. Don't they know we were just trying to correct THEIR mistake?

\>

FtLouie: Totally. How was your day?

\>

SkinnerBx: Great. Today in my Policymaking

137

Under Uncertainty seminar we talked about how satellite imaging has revealed that Yellowstone National Park is actually a massive caldera, or crater, formed by a supervolcano, which is basically an underground reservoir for magma that has blown every 600,000 years, and is now about 40,000 years late for eruption. Also that when it does blow, volcanic ash from the explosion would travel as far away as Iowa and the explosion would be 2,500 times more forceful than that of Mount St Helens, killing tens of thousands immediately, and then millions more in the resulting nuclear winter. Unless, of course, we can figure out a way to relieve some of the pressure now and prevent what could be a global disaster.

OK, I HAVE to say it. *What kind of school is Michael going to anyway?*

```
SkinnerBx: So are your mom and Mr G still going
           away this weekend?
>
FtLouie:   Yes. They're making me stay with
           GRANDMERE.
>
SkinnerBx: Harsh. Your own room?
>
```

```
FtLouie:    OF COURSE! Same floor though. I hope
            I won't still be able to hear her
            snore through the walls.
>
SkinnerBx:  Does your dad have bodyguards posted
            in the actual hallway on that floor?
            Or are they just in neighbouring
            rooms?
```

God, he asks the strangest questions sometimes. Boys
are so WEIRD.

```
FtLouie:    Lars and those guys stay on the
            floor below.
>
SkinnerBx:  Are there security cameras?
```

The Moscovitz family is totally security-camera para-
noid these days.

```
FtLouie:    No, there are no security cameras.
            Well, I mean the hotel probably has
            them. Like in *Maid in Manhattan*. But
            not the RGG.
```

(RGG is short for Royal Genovian Guard, which is what
Lars is a member of.)

```
FtLouie:    What's with all the questions any-
            way? You planning on sneaking up
            there to steal the crown jewels? You
            already have a moon rock. What more
            do you want? Ha ha.
```

```
>
SkinnerBx: Ha ha. Yeah, no, I was just won-
           dering. So you're still coming over
           Saturday, right?
>
FtLouie:   It is the only thing I have to look
           forward to in my WHOLE LIFE RIGHT
           NOW.
>
SkinnerBx: I know. I miss you too.
```

Awwwwwwwwwwwwwww. I mean, seriously. It may not be very feminist of me, but I love it when he says – or writes – stuff like this. Actually writing is better because then I have actual proof, you know. That he loves me.

Then I heard a familiar sound.

```
FtLouie:   Michael, I have to go. Rocky patrol.
>
SkinnerBx: Gotcha. Over and out.
```

You know, I really think Lana is wrong. Not ALL college boys expect their girlfriends to Do It. Because Michael hasn't said a SINGLE word to me about it.

And once after he paid for a couple of slices at Ray's Pizza he left his wallet on the table and I looked all through it – while he was in the men's room – because I was curious about what boys keep in their wallets, and here is what I found:

- Forty-eight dollars
- Metro card
- Hayden Planetarium membership card

- School ID
- Driver's licence
- Forbidden Planet Comic Superstore discount card
- NYC Public Library card

But no condom.

Which just goes to show my boyfriend clearly has other things on his mind than sex.

Such as the future energy crisis. And potential global disasters caused by supervolcanoes.

Which is a lot more than Lilly can say about Boris.

I mean Tina.

Whoever.

Maybe Michael and I won't ever even HAVE to have The Talk.

Friday, September 4, PE

I hate her so much.

Friday, September 4, Geometry

Seriously, where does she get off?

Theorem = statement that is proved by reasoning deductively from already accepted statements.

She only said it to get under my skin.
    Right?
    Because it can't be true. It CAN'T be.
    Can it?

Friday, September 4, English

What was THAT about?????

What? Oh, the pom-pom squeezy thing? What do I want with a stupid squeezy thing shaped like a pom-pom that says *Vote for Lana* on it? I hate Lana. Do you have any idea what she said to me today in PE? IN FRONT OF LILLY????

What?????

She said college boys whose girlfriends won't Do It with them dump them for girls who will.

SHE DID NOT.

Oh, yes, she did. Right there in the shower. Right in front of everyone. In front of Lilly. Who'll tell Michael now.

She won't! Why would she?

Because he's her brother.

She won't. Some things you don't tell your brother.
Believe me, Mia, I have a brother. I know.

Tina, your brother is six years old.

OK, but whatever. Lilly won't tell Michael.
Anyway . . . what did she say when she heard?

144

She told Lana to cram it up her gym shorts.

See??? I told you.

Still!!!! You know what ELSE she said? Lana, I mean.
She said boys HAVE to Do It, because if they don't it
all backs up in there and they go crazy.

Wait . . . what backs up in where?

YOU KNOW. Think Health and Safety. Last year.

EWWWWWWWWWWWWWW!!!!!!!!!!!!!!
And it doesn't. Back up, I mean. Or Coach
Wheeton would have said so.

But it would explain why boys whose girlfriends don't
Do It have to dump them and find girls who will.
Tina, what if it's true???? What if Lana knows some-
thing we don't know????

There's a simple way to find out.
Did you talk to Michael about it?

NOT YET!!! I TOLD YOU!!!!

Well, when you see him tomorrow you'll talk about
it and you'll realize—

CAN YOU BELIEVE SHE IS STANDING OUT THERE GIVING
AWAY THESE STUPID THINGS???? She must have spent a
FORTUNE on them. And look how cheap they are. You can scrape

the VOTE FOR LANA part right off. It's probably lead-based paint too, which is toxic. Anyway, Mia, don't feel inadequate. I put a call in to your grandmother and it's all under control. We're going to find something for you to give away too.

LILLY!!! I DON'T WANT TO GIVE ANYTHING AWAY!!! I DON'T EVEN WANT TO BE PRESIDENT!!!

Don't worry, you won't be.

YOU KEEP SAYING THAT, LILLY, AND YET EVERY TIME I TURN AROUND YOU'RE DOING SOMETHING ELSE TO HELP ME WIN, LIKE CALLING MY GRANDMOTHER AND GETTING HER TO GIVE AWAY FREE THINGS TO KIDS TO GET THEM TO VOTE FOR ME!!!!

Oooh, could you get Mia's grandma to give away free tiaras?
Because I would totally take one!

We can't give away tiaras, Tina. It's not in the budget.
I'm looking into tiara-shaped squeezy things like Lana has though.

WOULD YOU PLEASE LISTEN TO ME, LILLY????
I CAN'T TAKE THIS ANY MORE!!!! THE MADNESS HAS GOT TO STOP!!!!!!!!

Calm down, PIT. Everything's going to be all right. My brother's not going to dump you for not Doing It with him. At least, not if he wants to keep his stupid dog alive.

Whatever. Lana's on crack. Don't worry about it. You know Michael's not like that.

But he's in COLLEGE now, Lilly. He's CHANGING. Every time I talk to him he's learned some new, heinous thing. And what about . . . you know. THE BACK-UP.

Hello. It's the Ivy League. No one is having sex there. Believe me. Did you SEE those girls the day we went to help him move in? Um, hello, it's called shampoo. Try some.

It's true, Mia. You're MUCH cuter than all those genius Ivy League girls. Remember Elle's study group in *Legally Blonde*?

Can we please focus on what's important here? Tiara-shaped squeezy things. Yay or nay?

Oh my God. She's handing back my paper . . . and it's . . .

. . . covered in little red marks. Oh, Mia. I'm so sorry.
Mia? MIA?

Friday, September 4, nurse's office

I am lying here with a cool cloth over my forehead. Although it is very hard to write in your journal AND keep a cool cloth on your forehead, I am finding out.

The nurse says to try to keep still and not think so much. Ha! Who does that nurse think she's dealing with? It's ME, Mia Thermopolis! It is impossible for me not to think so much. Thinking is all I ever do.

Fortunately she can't see me disobeying her orders because she went into her cubicle to fill out some forms. Hopefully they're forms to have me committed. I can't debate Lana on Monday if I'm in a mental institution.

Nurse Lloyd says I'm not crazy though. She says everybody has their breaking point, and when I walked out into the hallway after receiving another B in English and saw my grandmother standing there in her tiara and ermine cape, handing out pens that say *Propriété du Palais Royale de Genovia* to everyone walking by, I reached mine.

Nurse Lloyd says it's not my fault I went mental, grabbed the box of pens out of Grandmere's hands and threw it at the security camera hanging outside the door to Principal Gupta's office.

The camera's not even broken. I mean, there are PENS all over the place.

But the camera is just fine.

I don't know why they had to call my mom and dad.

Nurse Lloyd says I should just rest quietly until they get here. She is keeping Grandmere out at my request. Not that it's Grandmere's fault really. I mean, she was just trying to help. Lilly must have called her and told her about Lana's pom-pom-shaped squeezy things. So

Grandmere felt obligated to rush over here with something she thought *I* could hand out.

Because who DOESN'T want a pen that says *Propriété du Palais Royale de Genovia* on it?

Really, none of this is anyone's fault. Except my own. I should never have handed that paper in to Ms Martinez. What was I THINKING? How could I for ONE MINUTE have thought that she would appreciate a paper comparing Romeo and Juliet's forbidden love with that of Britney Spears and Jason Allen Alexander? I mean, yeah, I poured my HEART and SOUL into it. I wanted the reader to feel Britney's pain at the way she and Jason were torn apart by the media and her management and record company. It's so clear to me that these two childhood sweethearts were meant for each other . . .

I should have known Ms Martinez wouldn't share my concern for Britney. It's quite clear she's never REALLY listened to 'Everytime'.

Oh no.

SOMEONE'S COMING!!! MUST GET CLOTH BACK ON HEAD!!!!

Friday, September 4, later, nurse's office

It was just my dad. I asked him how he got here so fast, and he said because he'd been on his way to the French mission to argue with them about voting Genovia out of the EU.

This just made me feel worse. Because it reminded me of how I'd let my own people down so very badly with the whole snail thing.

Dad said not to worry about it, that if anyone should be voted out of the EU it should be Monaco, for letting the museum, which was under Jacques Cousteau's supervision at the time, dump South American seaweed into the Mediterranean in the first place, and also France, for sitting on their hands about it for a decade afterwards.

I apologized to Dad for interrupting his busy day of politicking, but he just patted my hand and said everyone is entitled to a 'crying jag' now and then. I asked him if that was Nurse Lloyd's clinical diagnosis of what had happened to me and he said, 'Not exactly,' but that he's seen a lot of crying jags in his day. Although never in someone who hadn't had more Genovian prosecco than was good for her.

It's very embarrassing to blubber like a big baby in front of the whole school, not to mention doing it later in front of your dad. Especially when, you know, there's no Kleenex whatsoever around because I had used it all up already. So I had to blow my snot into my dad's silk show-hanky. Not that he looked like he minded too much. He'll probably just throw it away and buy a new one, like Britney Spears does with her underwear. It's nice to be a prince. Or a popstar.

Anyway, Dad was way concerned and kept asking me

what was wrong. *What's wrong, Dad?* Oh, you mean other than *everything*?

Of course the only thing I could TELL him about was the Ms Martinez thing. Because I knew if I told him about how much the whole election thing was bumming me out, he wouldn't understand and he'd just say something all fathery like, 'Oh, Mia, don't put yourself down. You know you'll do great.'

And God knows I couldn't tell him about the Michael thing. I mean, I love my dad. I don't want to cause his head to explode.

At first my dad totally didn't believe me. You know, that I could get a B on an English paper. I had to pull out my paper and SHOW him.

And then his eyes got all squinty – but I think mostly because he'd left his reading glasses back in the limo – and he cleared his throat a bunch of times.

Then he said some stuff about how *this* was what he was getting for his 20,000 dollars a year and what kind of world was it where a little girl's dream could get shot down like so much skeet, and that if this Ms Martinez person thinks she can get away with this, she has another think coming.

So, you know. That was kind of entertaining for a while: watching him hop around, all mad.

Finally the nurse heard him and she came in and shooed him out.

While Nurse Lloyd was shooing my dad out, though, my mom managed to sneak in, looking all flustered, with Rocky strapped to her. So I sat up and smelt his head for a while, because Rocky's head smells almost as good as Michael's neck, although in a much different way of course.

151

Although the smell of Rocky's head cannot soothe my fractious soul the way the smell of Michael's neck can.

While I smelt Rocky's head my mom said, 'Mia, this is a really bad time for you to have a breakdown. Our flight to Indiana leaves in two hours.'

I assured my mom that I wasn't having a breakdown, that it was just a crying jag. I didn't mention what had brought it on. You know, the part about what Lana had told me about college boys. And then Ms Martinez shooting down my dreams of being a writer. Instead I just said maybe I still had jet lag from my summer in Genovia and all.

'This isn't jet lag,' my mother said scornfully. 'This has Clarisse Renaldo written all over it.'

Well, I hadn't wanted to say so out loud. At least not to my mom, who has enough reasons not to like Grandmere.

But it IS true that the straw that broke the camel's back was seeing Grandmere passing out pens in the hallway.

'She means well,' I pointed out to my mom.

'Does she?' Mom looked dubious.

But I assured my mom that this time Grandmere had only the good of the crown at heart. After all, if my student-electoral campaign kept the press away from the story about Genovia being voted out of the EU, it was totally worth it.

Sort of.

Mom didn't look like she believed this though.

'Mia, if you want to quit this election thing, just say the word. I'll make it happen.'

My mom can look pretty fierce when she wants to – even with a baby as adorable as Rocky strapped to her chest. Really, if I had to make a choice between debating Lana and debating my mom about something, I'd pick Lana every time.

'No, Mom, it's OK,' I said. '*I'm* OK. Really. So . . . are you going to look up Wendell when you get back to Versailles?'

My mom was busy fussing with Rocky's foot, which had gotten all tangled up in the Tibetan prayer flags she had hanging from his carrier. 'Who?'

'Wendell Jenkins.' God! I can't believe she doesn't even remember the man to whom she gave the gift of the flower of her virginity. 'He still lives there. He and April. He works for the power company. And did you know April was a corn princess?'

Mom looked amused. 'Really? How do you know all this, Mia?'

'Yahoo! People search,' I said. 'If you run into April be sure to tell her, you know, how you're the mother of the princess of Genovia. That's a lot better than being a corn princess even if we ARE about to be thrown out of the EU.'

'I'll be sure to,' Mom said. 'You're positive you're going to be OK? Because I won't go to Versailles if you don't want me to.'

I assured Mom I would be fine. At which point Nurse Lloyd came back in and, finding my mother there, basically assured her of the same thing. Then, after letting Nurse Lloyd coo over Rocky for a while – because he is the cutest baby there ever was, and no one who sees him can HELP but coo over him – Mom left and I was all alone with Nurse Lloyd again.

Which, you know, reminded me that there was something I needed to know. And a member of the health profession was the perfect person to ask, since I couldn't go to Yahoo! Health as there wasn't a computer handy.

'Nurse Lloyd,' I said from around the thermometer she'd shoved under my tongue, to make sure I was well and truly cured and could be sent back to class.

'Yes, Mia?' She was looking at her watch as she took my pulse.

'Is it true that if college boys don't Do It it backs up?'

Nurse Lloyd snorted. 'Is that one still really going around? Mia, you should know better. You took Health and Safety, didn't you?'

'Then . . . it's not true?'

'It most certainly is not.' Nurse Lloyd let go of my wrist and took the thermometer out of my mouth. 'And don't let any of them try to tell you differently. And PS, any condom that's been in a wallet for an extended period of time should be discarded and replaced with a new one. Friction from movement while carrying the wallet in a pocket can cause tiny holes to develop in the latex.'

I just stared at her with my mouth hanging open. HOW HAD SHE KNOWN ABOUT THIS?

Nurse Lloyd just looked down at the thermometer and said, 'I've been in this job a long time. Oh, look, ninety-eight point six. You're cured. You can go now if you want. But before you do, Mia, just one more thing.'

I looked at her expectantly.

'You must stop bottling things up inside,' she said. 'I know you like to write a lot in your diary – yes, I've seen you – and that's great. But you've got to VERBALIZE your feelings as well. Especially if you're angry or upset with someone. The more you keep it buried inside, the more something like what happened today is going to happen. I know princesses are told to keep a stiff upper lip and all of that, but the truth is, if anyone shouldn't be letting things get backed up, it's you. Do you understand me?'

I nodded. Nurse Lloyd may be the smartest person I have ever met. And that includes all the geniuses I happen to be best friends with or go out with.

'Fine. Just let me write you a hall pass,' said Nurse Lloyd.

Which is what she's doing now.

Do you know what?

NURSE LLOYD IS THE BOMB!!!!!

Note to self: tell Tina to make Boris buy a new condom before they Do It on prom night.

Friday, September 4, third-floor stairwell

When I came out of the nurse's office Lilly was sitting there in the hallway, waiting for me. She had three detention slips in her hand because hall monitors had come around and found her there and written her up.

But she says she doesn't care because she HAD to make sure I was all right. She says she HAD to see me.

Remembering what Nurse Lloyd had said about not keeping things bottled up inside, I told Lilly I HAD to see her too.

So we escaped up here, where no one will find us, unless someone needs to get to the roof. But the only time anyone needs to do that is if some kid from the building next door has thrown his Pikachu or whatever out the window, on to the school's rooftop, and the custodian or the doorman from next door has to come up here to get it.

Anyway at first I have to admit I was kind of distant to Lilly because, hello, she is at least partially responsible for my crying jag. I mean, pens from the palace????

'But people love them,' was her big excuse. 'Seriously, Mia, people are, like, keeping them as souvenirs. Not everyone gets to go live in a castle every summer like you do.'

'That's not the point.' I can't believe that, even though Lilly is a genius and all, she needs to have stuff like this explained to her. 'The point is that you promised me I wouldn't have to go through with this.'

Lilly just blinked at me. 'When did I say that?'

'LILLY!' I couldn't believe it. 'You swore I wouldn't end up having to be Student Council President!'

'I know,' Lilly said. 'And you won't.'

'But you also promised me Lana wouldn't crush me in a humiliating defeat in front of everyone!'

'I know,' Lilly said. 'She won't.'

'LILLY!' I felt like the top of my head was going to blow off. 'If Lana doesn't beat me, I WILL be President.'

'No, you won't,' Lilly said. '*I* will.'

Now it was my turn to blink. 'WHAT? That doesn't make any sense.'

'Yes, it does,' Lilly said calmly. 'See, what's going to happen is, you're going to win the election – because you're a princess and you're nice to everyone and people like you. Then, after a suitable period of time – say two or three days – you're going to have to (regretfully, of course) step down from the presidency on account of being too busy with the whole princess thing. That is when I, whom you will have appointed your Vice-president, will have to assume the mantle of presidential responsibility.' Lilly shrugged. 'See? Simple.'

I stared at Lilly, completely dumbfounded.

'Wait a minute. You're doing all of this just so that YOU can be President?'

Lilly nodded.

'But, Lilly . . . why didn't you just run then?'

That's when something totally unexpected happened. Lilly's eyes, behind the lenses of her glasses, filled up with tears. Next thing I knew she was having a crying jag of her very own.

'Because there's no way I could ever win,' she said with a sob. 'Don't you remember how I got crushed in last year's election? Nobody likes me. Not the way they like you, Mia. I mean, you may be a baby-licker and all, but people seem to be able to relate to you, even with the whole princess thing. NOBODY can relate to me . . .

157

maybe because I'm a genius and that's intimidating to people or something. I don't know why really. I mean, you would think people would want the smartest leader they could find, but instead they seem perfectly content to elect total MORONS.'

I tried not to take Lilly's calling me a moron to heart. After all, she was in the middle of a full-blown personal crisis.

'Lilly,' I said in astonishment. 'I didn't know you thought of yourself that way. You know. As not popular.'

Lilly looked up from the detention slips she was weeping into.

'W-why w-would I ever consider myself popular?' she stammered sorrowfully. 'Y-you're the only real friend I've got.'

'That's not true,' I said. 'You have lots of friends, Shameeka and Ling Su and Tina—'

Lilly started to cry harder at the mention of Tina's name. Too late, I remembered Boris and his new hotness.

'Oh,' I said, patting Lilly on the shoulder. 'Sorry. What I meant was . . . Well, whatever. People DO like you, Lilly. It's just that sometimes . . .'

Lilly lifted her tear-stained face.

'W-What?' she asked.

'Well,' I said. 'Sometimes you're kind of mean to people. Like me. With the whole baby-licker thing.'

'But you ARE a baby-licker,' Lilly pointed out.

'Yes,' I said. 'But, you know, you don't need to SAY it all the time.'

Lilly rested her chin on her knees.

'I guess not,' she said with a sigh. 'You're right. I'm sorry.'

While I had her in a conciliatory mood, I added, 'And I don't like it when you call me POG or PIT either.'

Lilly looked at me blankly.

'Then what am I supposed to call you?'

'How about just plain Mia?'

Lilly seemed to think about this.

'But . . . that's so boring,' she said.

'But it's my name,' I pointed out.

Lilly sighed again.

'Fine,' she said. 'Whatever. You have no idea how good you have it, POG. I mean, Mia.'

'Good? *ME?* Please!' I practically burst out laughing. 'My life is TERRIBLE right now. Did you SEE what Ms Martinez gave me on my paper?'

Lilly wiped her eyes.

'Well, yeah,' she said. 'She WAS a little harsh. But a B isn't really that bad, Mia. Besides, I saw your dad heading towards her classroom a little while ago. He looked like he was going to read her the riot act.'

'Yeah, but what good is that going to do me?' I wanted to know. 'I mean, it's not going to change her mind about my writing talent . . . or lack thereof. It's just going to make her, you know, scared of my dad.'

Lilly just shook her head.

'Yeah,' she said. 'But at least you have a boyfriend.'

'Who's in COLLEGE,' I reminded her. 'And who apparently expects—'

'Oh, please,' Lilly said. 'Not that stupid Lana thing again. When are you going to get it through your head that Lana doesn't know what she's talking about? I mean, do you see HER dating a college boy?'

'No,' I said. 'But—'

'Yeah, well, there might be a REASON for that. And

if what it says all over the ladies'-room wall is true, it is NOT because Lana has any reservations about Doing It.'

We both sat there and thought about that for a while. Then Lilly said, 'So, are your mom and Mr G still going to Indiana for the weekend?'

'Yes,' I said and then added quickly, 'But there isn't going to be any party at my place because I'm staying at the Plaza.'

'In your own room?' Lilly asked. When I nodded, she said, 'Sweet.' Then she said, 'Hey, you should have a slumber party.'

I looked at her like she was crazy.

'At the *hotel*?'

'Sure,' Lilly said. 'It'll be fun. And we need to work on your debate skills anyway. We could do a mock run-through. How about it?'

'Well,' I said. 'I guess so.'

Although I'm not sure how Dad and Grandmere are going to feel about this. My having a slumber party at the Plaza.

But, oh well. If it'll make Lilly happy, I guess it's worth it. I seriously never knew she felt that way about herself. You know, that she's not popular. I mean, *I* know Lilly isn't very popular. But I never knew SHE knew it. She always ACTS like she thinks she's the queen of the school.

Who knew it was all for show?

Now we both have to sit here until the bell for sixth period rings and we can duck back downstairs and mingle with the rest of the hordes. We're missing Gifted and Talented, but I have my pass from the nurse to show Mrs Hill on Monday, so she won't count

160

me absent from today.

I don't know what Lilly's going to do about it. She doesn't seem to care all that much either. Really, if you think about it, Grandmere and Lilly could BOTH teach the world a thing or two about acting like a princess.

Which is kind of scary if you *do* think about it.

THEORIES OF GOVERNMENT (cont.)
EVOLUTIONARY THEORY:

Darwin theory of evolution – applied government =
1. Family
2. Clan
3. Tribe

Groups formed to coordinate and manage enterprise of goods and services.

To maintain internal order and protect from external danger, governmental institutions were formed.

(Wow, this is just like cliques! Seriously! I mean, the way cliques are formed within a school – to protect from external danger. Like, for instance, all of us Geeks bonded together and formed a clique to protect ourselves from being picked on by the Jocks and Cheerleaders because there is safety in numbers. This explains so much:

- The Sk8terbois' clique formed to protect them selves from the Punks
- The Punks formed to protect themselves from the Drama Club
- The Drama Club formed to protect themselves from the Nerds
- The Nerds formed together to protect themselves from the Jocks
- And the Jocks formed to protect themselves from . . .

Well, I don't know who the Jocks formed together to protect themselves from. But otherwise it's all making sense now. This is why cliques exist! Darwin was right!!!)

Friday, September 4, Earth Science

Magnetic field surrounding earth due to interior convection currents

    Discovered by Van Allen (radiation belts)

    High radiation zone due to particles, some radioactive and charged, from space and sun

    Aurora borealis caused by interaction of charged particles with the atmosphere

Kenny's new girlfriend Heather, according to Kenny:

1. Has naturally blonde hair and never needs to get her roots touched up
2. Gets straight As and is in all honours classes
3. Can do a back handspring
4. Often does them at parties
5. And in restaurants
6. Is totally popular at her school in Delaware
7. Is coming to see him at Thanksgiving
8. Has her own horse
9. Never wastes her time watching TV, because she is too busy reading books
10. Doesn't have an answering machine

Which is just as well, because probably no one ever wants to call her, since she doesn't watch TV and therefore has nothing to talk about.

PE:	N/A
Geometry:	Exercises, pages 42–45
English:	Strunk and White, pages 55–75
French:	????
Gifted and Talented:	????
US Government:	How is Darwin's theory applied to def. of gov.?
Earth Science:	Section 2, Nature of Energetic Environment

Friday, September 4, the Plaza

Grandmere felt so badly about having caused me to have a crying jag in the middle of the school day that she insisted on taking me to tea downstairs in the Palm to make up for it.

Of course I knew she didn't REALLY feel bad. I mean, she is GRANDMERE after all. And there WERE Press all over the place, trying to get pictures of us eating our scones with clotted cream so that tomorrow on the front of the *Post* there'll be a photo of us sitting there and a big headline that goes *Tea 4 2/Take that, EU!* or *FU, EU* or something.

But it *was* nice to sit there and eat tiny sandwiches with the crusts cut off while Grandmere nattered on about Lana's pom-pom-shaped squeezy things and how cheap they are and how much more superior our Propriété du Palais Royale de Genovia pens are. Especially, you know, since I hadn't had any lunch due to having spent all of that time in the nurse's office with a cool cloth on my forehead.

Grandmere was being so nice on account of the whole feeling-guilty thing (note to self: can someone with borderline personality disorder feel guilt? Check on this) that I finally just came out and went, 'Grandmere, can I have Lilly and Tina and Shameeka and Ling Su over for a slumber party in my room tonight, so we can do a mock debate?' and she went, totally calmly, 'Of course, Amelia.'

EEEEEEEEEEEEEEEEEEEEEEEEEEEEEEEE!!!!!!!!!!!!!!!!!!

So then I got on my cellphone and called them all and invited them. Mr Taylor had to speak to Grandmere before he would let Shameeka come, to make sure there was going to be adequate supervision and all, but Grandmere carried it off like a champ. By the time she handed the phone back to me Mr Taylor was asking if there was anything we wanted Shameeka to bring, like a popcorn popper or whatever.

But I assured him that the Plaza would see to all of our needs.

We sent Grandmere's maid back to the Loft to get my stuff and feed Fat Louie.

I hope he'll be all right on his own. It's going to be weird for him not to have Rocky around. He's got very used to licking all the leftover milk from Rocky's face every evening, as a sort of midnight snack.

Note to self:

Call Mom on cellphone as soon as her plane has landed and remind her to keep Rocky away from:

- hay threshers
- copperhead snakes (native to Indiana and highly poisonous)
- pitchforks
- black widow spiders (their bite is deadly to infants)
- unpasteurized milk (salmonella)
- Papaw's La-Z-Boy (Rocky could become wedged inside it and suffocate)
- farm animals (E. coli)
- Mamaw's tuna-potato-chip-macaroni casserole (it's just gross)
- the cellar (escapee from local mental institution could be hiding there)

Friday, September 4, Time ???? LATE!!!!!!!, the Plaza, room 1620

Oh my God, Ling Su found the coolest quiz online and brought it with her so that we can all do it and find out stuff about ourselves!!!!

QUIZ:

DO NOT CHEAT!!! NO reading ahead . . . just answer the questions in order!

First, get a pen and paper. When you choose names, make sure it's people you actually know. Go with your first instinct. DO THIS NOW!

1. First, write the numbers 1 through 11 in a column.
2. Beside numbers 1 and 2, write down any two numbers you want.
3. Beside the 3 and 7, write down the names of members of the opposite sex.
4. Write anyone's name (like friends or family) in the fourth, fifth and sixth spots.
5. Write down four song titles in 8, 9, 10 and 11.

DO THIS NOW, WITHOUT READING AHEAD TO THE ANSWERS!!!!!!!!

Mia Thermopolis's Answers:

1. Ten
2. Three
3. Michael Moscovitz
4. Fat Louie
5. Lilly Moscovitz

6. Rocky Thermopolis-Gianini
7. Kenny Showalter
8. 'Crazy in Love' – Beyoncé
9. 'Bootylicious' – Destiny's Child
10. 'Belle' – *Beauty and the Beast*
11. Theme song from *Friends*

Answer key:

1. You must tell (the numbers in spaces 1 and 2) people about this game.
2. The person in space 3 is the one that you love.
3. The person in 7 is one you like but can't work out.
4. You care most about the person you put in 4.
5. The person you name in number 5 is the one who knows you very well.
6. The person you name in 6 is your lucky star.
7. The song in 8 is the song that matches with the person in number 3.
8. The title in 9 is the song for the person in 7.
9. The tenth space is the song that tells you most about YOUR mind.
10. The eleventh answer is the song telling you how you feel about life.

Oh my God!!! THIS IS SO CRAZY!!!! IT'S ALL SO TRUE!!!!!!

Like Michael is totally the person I love! And Rocky is totally my lucky star! And Lilly is the person who knows me the best! And Fat Louie is the person (or cat) that I care about the most!

And I don't think I'll EVER figure out Kenny. 'Bootylicious' is an appropriate song for him, because one thing I *do* know: I don't think he's ready for this jelly.

And I am DEFINITELY 'Crazy in Love' with Michael! And the *Friends* theme song is TOTALLY my life: *Nobody told you life was gonna be this way* . . . Because nobody ever TOLD me I was going to be PRINCESS OF GENOVIA.

And as for the song 'Belle', Lilly can laugh all she wants, but it IS one of my favourite songs ever. And yeah, Ms Martinez would probably find that reprehesible . . . you know, a so-called writer liking a song from a Disney musical. But whatever! Belle and I have a LOT in common: we both always have our head in a book (well, mine's a journal, but whatever) and everyone thinks we're weird.

Except the men who love us.

Whatever. This is so much fun! We've ordered like EVERYTHING from room service. And a little while ago Lilly practically made us all wet ourselves from laughing so hard after Shameeka told her about Perin, from French, and how we can't tell if Perin is a boy or a girl, and Lilly said we should go into class on Monday and make a circle around Perin and chant, 'Pull . . . down . . . your . . . pants! Pull . . . down . . . your . . . pants!', so we could look and see.

Could you imagine the look on Mademoiselle Klein's face if we did that? Only, of course, I think that would be sexual harassment. And it wouldn't be very nice for Perin, that poor girl or boy.

So then we all jumped up and down on the bed and chanted, 'Pull . . . down . . . your . . . pants! Pull . . . down . . . your . . . pants!' at the top of our lungs until I thought I actually might WET my pants from laughing so hard.

Next, we're going to have a karaoke contest. Because

I told everyone about how if we are ever travelling across country and we have to sing for gas money and all, like Britney Spears in *Crossroads*, we'll need a good act. So we're gonna get on that right away.

Oh, and Michael called a minute ago, but I couldn't hear what he was saying on account of how Tina was screaming because we found a love note Boris left in her backpack and Ling Su was reading it out loud. Even Lilly was laughing.

This is the BEST NIGHT EVER. Except, of course, for the night of the Nondenominational Winter Dance.

And the night Michael and I watched *Star Wars* together and he told me he was IN love with me, not just loved me.

And the prom.

But except for those.

Note to self: remember to tell Mom to keep Rocky away from Papaw's chewing tobacco! Nicotine is toxic to babies if ingested! I saw it on *Law and Order*!

Lilly, Shameeka, Tina, Ling Su and Mia's List of Totally Hot Guys:

1. *Orlando Bloom, in anything, with or without shirt on.*
2. *Boris Pelkowski* (This is so WRONG! Boris should NOT be on this list. But Lilly and I were outvoted.)
3. *The cute guy from the most recent movie of Mia's life* (except that none of what happened in that movie could ever happen in real life since Genovia is a principality not a monarchy and it doesn't matter if the heir is married or not. Plus Skinner Box is unlikely to get a record deal since most of its members are too busy getting college degrees/thirty-day sobriety chips to practise).

4. *Seth from* The OC.
5. *Harry Potter* (Because even though he's still only four-teen or whatever, he's getting kind of hot.)
6. *Enrique Iglesias, now that he's had that mole removed.*
7. *Chad Michael Murray from* Freaky Friday *and* One Tree Hill. *Ooooh la la.*
8. *Samantha's hot boyfriend on* Sex and the City, *particularly when he shaved his head for her* (Shameeka had to abstain from voting on this one since her dad won't let her watch this show).
9. *Poor Jason Allen Alexander, Mr Britney Spears.*
10. *Ramon Rivera.*

Saturday, September 5, 1 p.m., the Great Lawn, Central Park

I'm so tired. WHY did I invite everybody over last night? And WHY did we stay up singing karaoke until 3 a.m.????

More to the point, WHY did I let Lilly talk me into going to an Albert Einstein High School SOCCER game today????

It's so boring. I mean, I've always thought sports were boring – God knows, Mrs Potts has yelled, 'Let's see some hustle, Mia!' at me enough times when I've let balls bounce right past me.

But *watching* sports is even more boring than *playing* them. At least when you're playing sports you get those sweaty-palmed, heart-pounding moments of, *Oh no! The ball's not coming towards ME, is it? Oh no. It IS coming towards me. What do I do? If I try to catch it I'll miss and everyone will hate me. But if I DON'T try to catch it everyone will hate me for THAT too.*

But when you're WATCHING sports there's none of that. There's just . . . boredom. Seemingly never-ending boredom.

When Lilly asked me to keep Saturday during the day free for her, I didn't know she meant so we could go to a school-related event. Why would I want to do school stuff (besides homework, I mean) on a WEEKEND?

But Lilly says it's important that I show myself at as many school functions as possible before the election on Monday. She keeps poking me and going, 'Stop writing in your journal and go mingle.'

But I'm not actually so sure mingling at a school soccer game is the way to get votes. You know? Because it's pretty much guaranteed that everyone here is going to vote for Lana.

And why SHOULDN'T they? Look at her over there, doing all those basket tosses or whatever. She's totally PERFECT. On the outside anyway. Inside, I know her heart is black as pitch and all. But outside – well, she's got that perfect smile with those perfect, gap-free teeth, and those perfectly smooth tanned legs with no razor nicks, and that shiny lipgloss her hair never gets stuck to – why WOULD anyone vote for me when they could vote for Lana?

Lilly says not to be stupid – that the election for Student Council President isn't a beauty or popularity contest. But then how come she wants ME to run in her place? And how come I'm HERE? The only people AT this game are the other jocks and cheerleaders. And none of them are likely to vote for ME.

Lilly says they for sure won't vote for me if I don't get my nose out of this book and go talk to them. TALK TO THEM? THE PERFECT, POPULAR PEOPLE?

They'll be lucky if I don't BARF on them.

Saturday, September 5, 3 p.m., Ray's Pizza

Well, THAT was a big waste of time.

Lilly says it wasn't. Lilly says that, actually, the day was extremely EDUCATIONAL. Whatever that means.

I'm not sure how Lilly would even KNOW this since she spent almost the entire game sitting behind Dr and Mrs Weinberger – who were in the stands – eavesdropping on their conversation with Trisha Hayes's parents. She didn't even WATCH the game so far as I know. *I* was the one who had to wander around, going up to people who wouldn't have looked twice at me if we'd passed in the hallway at AEHS, and going, 'Hi, we haven't met. I'm Mia Thermopolis, Princess of Genovia, and I'm running for Student Council President.'

Seriously. I have never felt like a bigger dork.

Nobody paid the least bit of attention to me either. The game was apparently a super-exciting one. We were playing the Trinity varsity men's team, who have basically kicked our butts every single year in, like, the history of AEHS soccer or something.

But not today. Because today AEHS produced its secret weapon: Ramon Riveras. Basically, once Ramon got hold of the ball it pretty much never left his feet, except when he was kicking it past the Trinity goalie into the big netty thing. AEHS beat Trinity four to nothing.

And it turned out I was right about Ramon. He fully whipped his shirt off and threw it into the air after the winning goal. I don't want to start a rumour or anything, but I saw Mrs Weinberger sit up a little straighter when that happened.

And of course Lana went running out on to the field and fell into Ramon's arms. The last time I saw her that

174

day, he was carrying her around on his shoulders as if she were a trophy or something. For all I know, maybe she is: Win a game for AEHS, get one cheerleader, free.

Whatever. Ramon can have her. Maybe he'll keep her busy enough for her to leave ME alone. Me and my 'college boy'.

Which reminds me. I'm supposed to go over to Michael's dorm room after this, to meet his room-mate and 'catch up', since we haven't seen each other all week.

At least that's what Michael *said* we were going to do, when we managed to get hold of each other, earlier today. He sounded kind of annoyed when I finally remembered to turn my cellphone on and he got through at last.

'What was going on last night when I called?' he wanted to know.

'Um,' I said. I was kind of in the middle of buying a pretzel from one of those carts in the park when he called. A lot of people don't know this, but New York City pretzels – the kind you buy from a vendor on the street – have healing properties. It's true. I don't know what's in them, but if you buy one when you have a headache or whatever, as soon as you bite into one your headache goes away. And I had a pretty big headache on account of not having had any sleep.

'I had the girls over,' I explained to Michael, once I'd swallowed my first bite of hot, salty pretzel. 'For a sleepover. Only, you know, there wasn't much sleeping.' And I told him how we jumped on the bed screaming, 'Pull . . . down . . . your . . . pants,' and all.

Only Michael didn't seem to think it was very funny. Of course I didn't mention the part about how later I sang 'Milkshake' into the TV remote for everyone while wearing the rubber shower mat as a minidress. I mean, I don't want him to think I am completely INSANE.

'You have a hotel suite all to yourself,' was all Michael said, 'and you invite my sister over.'

'And Shameeka and Tina and Ling Su,' I said, wiping mustard from my chin. Because you have to put mustard on your pretzel or the healing properties don't work.

'Right,' Michael said. 'Well, are you going to come over here later or not?'

Which some people might have found kind of, you know, rude. Except to me, the fact that Michael was annoyed with me – for whatever reason – was kind of a relief. Because if he was annoyed with me, it probably meant that Doing It wasn't foremost in his mind. And I really wasn't looking forward to having the Doing It conversation, even though I knew Tina was right and we were going to have to get that out in the open one of these days.

So now I'm just having a restorative slice of plain-cheese pizza with Lilly before I summon up my strength to get into the limo with Lars and head uptown to Michael's dorm. Really, after an evening of partying, it is very difficult to function the next day. I don't know how those Hilton sisters do it.

Lilly is now saying that we have this election in the bag. I don't have the slightest idea what she's talking about since

a) We never did end up doing that mock-debate thingy last night, so it's not like I ever had a chance to brush up on my answers for Monday, and

176

b) Most of the people I talked to in the stands at the game today just looked at me like I was a mental case and went, 'I'm voting for Lana, dawg.'

But whatever. Lilly spent the entire game sitting with people's PARENTS, so what does she even know?

I wish I could ask her about this Doing It thing though. I mean, Lilly's never Done It either . . . at least I don't think so. She only got to second base with her last boyfriend.

Still, I'm sure she'd have some valuable insights into the whole thing.

But I can't talk to Lilly about Doing It or not Doing It with her BROTHER. I mean, GROSS. If any girl wanted to talk to me about Doing It with Rocky, I would probably punch her lights out. Although he is, of course, my *younger* brother and only five months old.

Besides, I think I kind of know what Lilly would say: Go for it.

Which is very easy for Lilly to say, because she is very at ease in her body. She doesn't, like I do, change out of her school uniform and into her gym shorts as fast as possible before and after PE, and in the darkest, emptiest corner of the room she can find. She has even, upon occasion, strutted around the locker room COMPLETELY naked, going, 'Does anyone have any deodorant I can borrow?' And the remarks Lana and her friends make concerning Lilly's pot belly and cellulite seem not to bother her in the least.

Not that I'm worried Michael's going to make remarks about my nude body. I'm just not so sure I'm comfortable with him knowing anything about it at all.

Although I wouldn't mind, of course, seeing his.

Probably this means I'm inhibited and a prude and sexist and everything bad. Probably I don't deserve to be President of the Albert Einstein Student Council, even if only for a couple of days before I resign and let Lilly take over. Certainly I don't deserve to be princess of a country which I have managed to get thrown out of the EU . . . well, if it comes to that anyway.

Really, I don't deserve much of anything.

Well, I guess I'll go to Michael's now.

Someone, please shoot me.

Saturday, September 5, 5 p.m., Michael's dorm-room bathroom

OK, I thought Columbia was a hard school to get into. I thought they actually screened their applicants.

So what are they doing letting crazy people like Michael's room-mate in here?

Everything was going fine until HE showed up. Lars and I buzzed Michael from the lobby of Engle Hall, which is Michael's dorm, and Michael came down to sign us in, because they take their students' safety very seriously here at Columbia University. I had to leave my student ID at the security desk, so I wouldn't try to leave the building without signing out. Lars had to leave his gun permit (although they let him keep his gun when they found out I was the Princess of Genovia and he was my bodyguard).

Anyway, once we were all signed in Michael took us upstairs. I had been in Engle Hall before, of course, the day he moved in, but it looks very different now that all the moving carts and parents are gone. There were people running around in just towels up and down the hallway, screaming, just like on *Gilmore Girls*! And very loud music was blaring out of some open doorways. There were posters everywhere urging residents to come to this or that protest march, and invitations to poetry readings at various nearby coffee houses. It was all very collegiate!

Michael seemed to have got over being annoyed with me, since he gave me a very nice kiss hello, during which I got to smell his neck and immediately felt better about things. Michael's neck is almost as good as an NYC vendor pretzel, as far as healing properties go.

Anyway, we managed to ditch Lars in the student lounge on Michael's floor as there was a baseball game on the big TV there. You would think Lars would have had enough athletics for one day, seeing as how we'd just spent like three hours at one sporting event, but whatever. He took one look at the score, which was tied, and was glued to the set, along with a number of other people who were as slack-jawed as he was.

Michael went ahead and took me to his room, which looks a lot better than it did the last time I'd seen it, the day he'd moved in. There's a map of the galaxy covering most of the cinderblock, more computer equipment than they probably have at NORAD, covering every available flat surface (not counting the beds), and a big sign that says *Don't Even THINK About Parking Here* on the ceiling that Michael swears he didn't steal off the street.

Michael's side of the room is very tidy, with a dark-blue comforter over the bed and a tiny fridge as a nightstand and CDs and books EVERYWHERE.

The other side of the room is a little messier, with a red comforter, a microwave instead of a fridge and DVDs and books EVERYWHERE.

Before I even had a chance to ask where Doo Pak was and when I was going to get to meet him, Michael pulled me down on to his bed. We were getting very nicely reacquainted after our week apart when the door opened suddenly and a tall Korean boy in glasses came in.

'Oh, hi, Doo Pak,' Michael said very casually. 'This is my girlfriend, Mia. Mia, this is Doo Pak.'

I held out my right hand and gave Doo Pak my best princess smile.

'Hello, Doo Pak,' I said. 'It's very nice to meet you.'

But Doo Pak didn't take my hand and shake it. Instead he looked from Michael to me and back again very quickly. Then he laughed and said, 'Ha ha, that is very funny! How much is he paying you to play this joke on me, huh?'

I looked at Michael all confused, and he said, 'Uh, Doo Pak, I'm not joking. This really is my girlfriend.'

Doo Pak just laughed some more and said, 'You Americans are always playing jokes! Really, you can stop now.'

So then I tried.

'Um,' I said. 'Doo Pak, I really am Michael's girl-friend. My name's Mia Thermopolis. It's nice to finally meet you. I've heard a lot about you.'

This is when Doo Pak began laughing so hard that he doubled up and fell over on to his bed.

'No,' he said, shaking his head as tears of laughter streamed down his face. 'No, no. This is not possible. *You* . . .' He pointed at me. '. . . cannot be going out with *him*.' And he pointed at Michael.

Michael was kind of starting to look irritated.

'Doo Pak,' he said, in the same warning voice I've heard him use with Lilly when she starts in on him about his fondness for *Star Trek: Enterprise*.

'Seriously,' I said to Doo Pak, trying to help, even though I didn't have the slightest idea what was so funny. 'Michael and I have been going out for over nine months. I go to Albert Einstein High School, which is just down the street, and live with my mother and step-dad down in the Vill—'

'You stop talking now, please,' Doo Pak said to me – very politely, I have to admit. But still. It's kind of weird

181

to be told to stop talking. Especially when Doo Pak then turned his back on me and started talking to Michael in a very urgent, low voice, and Michael responded in an equally low, but more annoyed than urgent voice.

It is extremely weird to be standing in a room watching two people have an urgent and annoyed conversation that you can't even eavesdrop on. So I went into the bathroom to give them some privacy.

I can hear Doo Pak whispering very urgently to Michael, who fortunately has stopped whispering his responses, so I can at least hear HIS part of the conversation.

'Doo Pak, I TOLD you who she is,' he just said. 'She's my GIRLFRIEND. Nobody is trying to play a joke on you.'

You know, their bathroom is actually quite clean, for boys. There's nothing in here I'm actually afraid to touch. I see they've exchanged the institutional rubber shower curtain for one with a map of the world on it. That must be to comfort Doo Pak, who clearly misses his native land. This way he can take a shower and gaze at his home country the whole time.

Oooooh, Doo Pak isn't whispering any more now either. They must both think I'm completely DEAF.

'But I don't understand, Mike,' Doo Pak is saying. MIKE????? 'Why would SHE go out with YOU?'

It's all becoming clearer now. Doo Pak must have recognized me. I *have* been in the press quite a lot lately on account of the whole snail thing and the election and all. Maybe he can't believe Michael is actually dating a princess.

I can't say I blame him. There really isn't anything in the world quite as dorky as being a princess. No wonder

Michael didn't warn him ahead of time. It must be excruciatingly embarrassing for him to have to admit to his college friends that not only is he dating a high-school girl, but she's also a PRINCESS.

Poor Michael. I never knew people actually TEASED him about the fact that he goes out with a royal. That, on top of the fact that his girlfriend has a bodyguard, is mammary-challenged and a baby-licker, makes Michael's devotion to me all the more extraordinary.

Ooooh, they've stopped talking. Maybe it's safe to come out now . . .

Saturday, September 5, 7 p.m., Cafe (212), John Jay Lerner Hall

I have to write this fast, while Michael is up paying for the food. Fortunately there's a horrendously long line at the cash register – this place is PACKED – so it should take him a while.

Anyway, I found out the reason Doo Pak thought Michael was pulling his leg about me being his girlfriend. And it has nothing to do with me being a princess. It has to do with Doo Pak thinking I'm too PRETTY for Michael.

I am not even kidding. Doo Pak told me so himself when I came out of the bathroom. He looked totally ashamed of himself. And he said, without Michael even hitting him first or anything, 'I am very sorry I did not believe you when you said you were Mike's girlfriend. You see,' he went on, in the same apologetic tone, 'you are much too pretty to be dating Mike. He is – what do you call it? Oh, yes – a nerd. Like me. And nerds like us don't get pretty girlfriends. So I thought he was pranking me. Please accept my very humble apologies for my mistake.'

I looked from Michael to Doo Pak to see if they were, um, pranking me, but I could tell from Doo Pak's red, embarrassed face and Michael's even *redder*, *more* embarrassed face that Doo Pak was telling the truth: he thinks I'm too pretty to go out with Michael!!!!! SERIOUSLY!!!!!!

They must have very different standards of prettiness in South Korea than they have here in the US.

Also, apparently, where Doo Pak is from, boys who play with computers all day just don't get girlfriends. At all.

Maybe this is why they are always drawing them. You know, through anime and manga.

But, as I explained to Doo Pak, being a nerd in America is actually quite stylish, and most sensible girls WANT to date a nerd – as opposed to a Jock or a Playa.

Doo Pak didn't look as if he dared believe me, but I pointed out that Bill Gates, who, of course, is the King of the Nerds, is in fact married. And that seemed to cinch it for him. He shook my hand and asked very excitedly whether I had any female friends I might bring over someday for him and the rest of the boys on the floor to meet.

I told him that I would certainly try.

Then Doo Pak excused himself to go to the computer store to buy the latest version of Myst, and Michael said irritably that he wished they would let freshmen have single rooms in the dorm, instead of forcing them to share with a room-mate.

Which reminds me about something I noticed in their bathroom right before Doo Pak let me out. Something that completely didn't register until JUST NOW. SOMETHING THAT MAY PERMANENTLY BURN ITSELF INTO THE SOFT TISSUE OF MY BRAIN:

THERE IS A BOX OF CONDOMS IN MICHAEL AND DOO PAK'S MEDICINE CABINET!!!!!!!!!!!!!

Seriously. I SAW it. Oh my God, I TOTALLY SAW IT.

WHAT DOES THIS MEAN???? I mean, clearly DOO PAK isn't Doing It with anyone. I mean, he basically ADMITTED he's never had a girlfriend.

So whose condoms ARE those?????

Ooops, 'Mike' is back . . .

Sunday, September 6, 1 a.m., limo back to the Plaza

OII MY GOD. OH MY GOD OH MY GOD OH MY GOD. I just have to breathe. Really. Like they made me do in yoga that one time. In. Out. In. Out.

OK. I can do this. I can write this. I can just set it down on paper like I do every other little thing that happens to me, and then it will be all right. It HAS to be all right. It just HAS to.

We did it.

We had The Talk.

AND MICHAEL EXPECTS US TO HAVE SEX . . .

. . . SOMEDAY.

There. I wrote it.

So why don't I feel any better??????

Oh God, what am I going to DO???? How could it turn out that Lana is right? Lana has never been right about ANYTHING!!! I remember she told us if you sneezed and held your nose at the same time your eardrums would explode. And what about the great 'If you take a shower while you have your period, you could bleed to death' rumour she started? Even last year she had a couple of people going with the whole aspirin + Diet Coke = hole in your stomach thing.

The point is, none of those turned out to be true.

Why did THIS one have to be the one she was telling the truth about?????

College boys DO expect their girlfriends to Do It. At least, eventually. I mean, Michael was very sweet and understanding and almost as embarrassed as I was about it. It's not like, you know, he's going to dump me if we don't Do It tomorrow or whatever.

But he's DEFINITELY interested in Doing It.

Someday.

AAAAAAAAAAAAARRRRRGGGHHHHH!!!!!!!!!!

I should have known of course. Because real men –
like the *X-men*'s Wolverine and the Beast from *Beauty
and the Beast* – ALL want to Do It. They may, you know,
be polite about it. I mean, Wolverine might engage in
witty repartee with Jean Gray while he lets Cyclops
slobber all over her.

And the Beast might whirl Belle around that ball-
room as if there is nothing on his mind but doing the
box step.

But there is no getting around the fact that ultimately,
deep down inside, ALL GUYS WANT TO DO IT.

I don't know why I thought Michael might be different. I mean, I have seen *Real Genius* and *Revenge of the
Nerds*. I should know perfectly well that even smart boys
like sex. Or *would* like it if they could find someone willing to have it with them.

And it's not like either of us belongs to a religion
where it's, like, against the law to Do It before you get
married or whatever. Well, I mean, Michael's Jewish but
he's not THAT Jewish. He eats BLTs all the time.

Still. I mean, SEX. That is a BIG step.

Which is what I said to Michael when we were making
out in his room after dinner tonight. Not like, you know,
he Made a Grab or anything. He's never done that –
although now I know he's WANTED to. It's just, you
know, that someone's always around. Except for tonight,
because Lars was totally glued to the TV in the lounge
with the rest of the sports freaks. And Doo Pak had gone
to the library to see if he could find any girls who might
be looking for a nerd-for-the-night.

But we came in from dinner and Michael put on some retro Roxy Music and pulled me on to his bed and we were kissing and stuff, and all I could think was, THERE ARE CONDOMS IN HIS MEDICINE CABINET and COLLEGE BOYS EXPECT THEIR GIRLFRIENDS TO DO IT and WENDELL JENKINS and CORN PRINCESS, and I couldn't concentrate on kissing and finally I just pulled away from him and went, 'I AM NOT READY TO HAVE SEX.'

Which I have to say seemed to surprise him very much.

Not the part about me not being ready, but the part about even mentioning it.

Still, he seemed to get over it pretty quickly, because after blinking a few times he just went, 'OK,' and went straight back to kissing me.

But this wasn't very reassuring because I couldn't tell if he'd really heard me or not. And besides, Tina had said Michael and I really needed to have The Talk about this, and I figured if she could talk to *Boris* about it I should be able to talk to Michael.

So I pushed him away again and said, 'Michael, we need to talk.'

He looked at me all confused and went, 'About what?'

And I said – EVEN THOUGH IT WAS THE HARDEST THING I'VE EVER DONE, EVEN HARDER THAN THE TIME I HAD TO ADDRESS THE GENOVIAN PARLIAMENT ON THE PARKING-METER ISSUE – 'The condoms in your medicine cabinet.'

And he said, 'The what?' And his eyes seemed all swirly and unfocused. Then he seemed to remember and went, 'Oh, those. Yeah. Everybody got them. As we were moving in. They were in that welcome pack they

188

handed everyone at check-in.'

And then his eyes seemed to get VERY focused – like laser beams – and he pointed them at me and went, 'But even if I'd bought them, what's the big deal? Is it wrong that I care about you and would want to protect you in the event we do make love?'

Which of course made me feel all melty inside, and it was VERY hard to remember that we were supposed to be having The Talk and not making out, especially when it occurred to me that:

As good as Michael's neck smells, the rest of him might smell EVEN BETTER.

Which is all the more reason why I knew we had to hurry up and have The Talk.

'No,' I said, moving his hand away from mine, because I knew it would be even harder to concentrate on having The Talk if he was touching me. 'I think that's a good thing. It's just that . . .'

And then it all came spilling out. What Lana had said in the jet line. Wendell Jenkins. What Lana had said in the shower (not the part about it backing up though. That was too gross). Corn princess. The fact that I love him but I'm not sure I'm ready to Do It yet (*I said* wasn't sure but, of course, I AM sure. I just, you know, didn't want to sound too harsh). The fact that condoms break (if it happened on *Friends* it could happen in real life). My mother's excessive fertility probably being an inheritable genetic tendency. EVERYTHING.

Because, you know, when you're having The Talk you have to put it ALL out there or what's the point?

Well, *almost* all of it anyway. I kind of left out the part about how I'm not so jazzed about the whole nudity thing. Well, MY nudity. His I'd be totally fine with. Plus, you know, on TV sex looks kind of . . . well, difficult. What if I mess it up? Or turn out not to be good at it? He might dump me.

Only, you know. I didn't mention any of that or anything.

Michael listened to the whole speech with a very serious look on his face. He even, at one point, got up to turn the music down. It was only when I got to the part about not being sure I was ready to Do It yet that he finally said something, and that was, in a very dry tone, 'Well, that's not actually a big surprise to me, Mia.'

Which was a surprise to ME anyway.

I went, 'Really?'

He said, 'Well, you made it fairly obvious where things stood when you invited all of your girlfriends, and not me, over the minute you found out you had a hotel room all to yourself for the weekend.'

HELLO. This is so not true. First of all, Lilly and those guys invited THEMSELVES over. And secondly—

Well, OK, he was right about this part.

'Michael,' I said, feeling completely horrible. 'I'm so, so sorry. I never even – I mean, I didn't even . . .'

I felt so awful I couldn't even VERBALIZE it. I felt like a total jerk. Kind of, like, how I felt at dinner when Michael was talking about his Sociology in Science Fiction class, and how in Orwell's *1984* the lottery is used as a way to control the masses, giving them false hope that they might one day be able to leave their dead-end jobs, and how in *Fahrenheit 451* Montague's wife is totally unsympathetic to his problems with setting books on fire for a living and how all she ever does is talk on the phone with her friends about some fictional TV show called *The White Clown*. I couldn't help remembering that all Lilly and Tina and I ever talk about half the time is *Charmed*.

But, hello, how can you NOT talk about that show?

But maybe that's all part of the government's strategy to keep us from noticing what they're up to with the clear-cutting of the national forests and the passing of laws that keep teens from being able to seek reproductive health care without their parents' consent . . .

Besides sometimes I think Michael won't ever stop talking about the shows he likes, like *Jake 2.0* and, lately, *60 Minutes*.

Anyway I did my best to make it up to Michael about the whole not-inviting-him-over-to-the-hotel thing. I put my hand on his and gazed deeply into his eyes and said, 'Michael, I really am sorry. Not just about that either. But the whole . . . well, everything.'

But instead of saying he forgave me or anything like that, Michael just went, 'Fine. The question is, when ARE you going to be ready?'

And I was like, 'Ready for what?'

And he said, 'It.'

It took me a minute to figure out what he meant.

And then, when it finally dawned on me, I turned bright red.

'Um,' I said.

Then I thought fast.

'How about after the prom,' I said, 'on a king-sized bed with white-satin sheets in a deluxe suite with Central Park views at the Four Seasons, with champagne and chocolate-covered strawberries upon arrival and an aromatherapy bath for after, then waffles for two in bed the next morning?'

To which Michael replied, very calmly, 'One, I'm never going to the prom again and you know it, and two,

I can't afford the Four Seasons – which you also know. So why don't you give that answer another try?'

Damn! Tina is so LUCKY to have a boyfriend she can push around. WHY isn't Michael as malleable as BORIS?

'Look,' I said, desperately trying to think of some way to get out of the whole situation. Because it wasn't going AT ALL the way I'd planned it in my head. In my head, I told Michael I wasn't ready to Do It and he said OK and we played some Boggle and that was the end of it.

Too bad things never work out the way they do inside my head.

'Do I have to decide this right NOW?' I asked, deciding DELAY was the best strategy at this point. 'I have a lot on my mind. I mean, it's possible that at this very moment my mom could be exposing Rocky to some very harmful stimuli, such as clog dancing or even funnel cakes. And I have this debate thing on Monday . . . did I mention that Grandmere and Lilly are working on it together? I mean, it's like Darth Vader joining forces with Ann Coulter. I'm telling you, I'm a wreck. Can I take a rain check on this whole thing?'

'Absolutely,' Michael said, with a smile that was so sweet it made me want to lean over to kiss him . . .

Until he added, 'But just so you know, Mia, I'm not going to wait around forever.'

This caused me to pause just as my lips were on the way to his.

Because he didn't mean that he wasn't going to wait around forever for my answer. Oh no. He meant he wasn't going to wait around forever to Do It.

He didn't say it like it was a threat or anything. He said it kind of lightly, even jokingly.

But I could tell it wasn't really a joke. Because boys really do expect you to Do It. Someday.

I didn't know what to say. Actually I don't think I could have spoken after that if I'd tried. Fortunately I didn't have to, because there was a knock on the door and Lars's voice called, 'The game is over. It's after midnight. Time to go, Princess,' which, of course, caused Michael and me to spring to separate sides of the room.

(I just asked Lars how he has such an uncanny knack for picking the wrong – or right, as the case may be – moment to interrupt me when I'm alone with Michael, and he went, 'As long as I hear voices I'm not worried. It's when things get quiet I start to wonder what's going on. Because – no offence, Your Highness – but you talk a *lot*.')

Anyway. So that's it.
Lana was right.
All boys want to Do It.
Including Michael.
My life is over.

The end.

Note to self: call Mom and remind her that she is still breastfeeding and that even though she might FEEL like drinking a lot of gin and tonics, seeing as how she's around her mother, this could be very dangerous to Rocky's cognitive development at this point.

Sunday, September 7, noon, my room, the Plaza

Why can't my life be like the lives of the kids on The N? None of them are princesses. None of them created eco-disasters in their native lands by pouring 10,000 snails into the local bay. None of them have boyfriends who expect them to Do It someday. Well, actually, some of them do.

But still. It's different when you're on TV.

Sunday, September 7, 1 p.m., my room, the Plaza

Why won't everyone leave me alone? If I want to wallow in my own grief, that should be my prerogative. After all, I AM a princess.

Sunday, September 7, 2 p.m., my room, the Plaza

I so wish I could talk to Michael right now. He called earlier, but I didn't pick up. He left a message with the hotel operator that said, 'Hey, it's me. Are you still there or have you gone home yet? I'll try you there too. Anyway if you get this message, call me.'

Yeah. Call him. So he can break up with me for my reluctance to Do It with him. I'm so not giving him the satisfaction.

I tried calling Lilly, but she's not home. Dr Moscovitz said she has no idea where her daughter is, but that if I hear from her I should let her know that Pavlov needs walking.

I hope Lilly isn't trying to secretly film through the windows of the Sacred Heart Convent again. I know she's convinced those nuns are running an illegal methamphetamine lab in there, but it was kind of embarrassing the last time, when she sent the video footage to the Sixth Precinct and all it turned out to have on it was shots of the nuns playing Bingo.

Oooooh, a *Sailor Moon* marathon . . .

Sailor Moon is so lucky to be a cartoon character. If I were a cartoon character I'm sure I would have none of the problems I am having right now.

And even if I did they would all be solved by the end of the episode.

Sunday, September 6, 3 p.m., my room, the Plaza

OK, this is just a violation of my personal rights. I mean, if I want to wallow in bed all day I should be allowed to. If that's what SHE felt like doing, and I went barrelling into HER private room and told her to stop feeling sorry for herself and sat down and started yammering away at her, you can bet SHE never would have gone along with it. She'd just have thrown a Sidecar at me or whatever.

But somehow it's all right for HER to do that to me. Come barrelling into my room, I mean, and tell me to stop feeling sorry for myself.

Now she's dangling this gold necklace in front of me. It's got a pendant almost as big as Fat Louie's head swinging from it. There are jewels all over the pendant. It looks like something 50 Cent might wear on his night off while he's working out or just hanging with his homies or something.

'Do you know what you are looking at here, Amelia?' Grandmere is asking me.

'If you're trying to hypnotize me into not biting my nails any more, Grandmere,' I said, 'it won't work. Dr Moscovitz already tried.'

Grandmere ignored that.

'What you are looking at here, Amelia, is a priceless artifact of Genovian history. It belonged to your namesake, St Amélie, the beloved patron saint of Genovia.'

'Um, sorry, Grandmere,' I said. 'But I was named after Amelia Earhart, the brave aviatrix.'

Grandmere snorted.

'You most certainly were not,' she said. 'You were named after St Amélie and no one else.'

197

'Um, excuse me, Grandmere,' I said. 'But my mom very definitely told me—'

'I don't care what that mother of yours told you,' Grandmere said. 'You were named after the patron saint of Genovia, pure and simple. St Amélie was born in the year 1070, a simple peasant girl whose greatest love was tending to her family's flock of Genovian goats. As she tended her father's herd, she often sang traditional Genovian folk songs to herself in a voice that was rumoured to be one of the loveliest, most melodic of all time, much nicer than that horrible Christina Aguilera person you seem to like so much.'

Um, hello. How does Grandmere even know this? Was she alive in the year 1070? Besides, Christina has like a seven-octave range. Or something like that.

'One fine day when Amélie was fourteen years old,' Grandmere went on, 'she was guarding the herd near the Italian/Genovian border when she happened to spy, billeted in a copse, an Italian count and the army of hired mercenaries he'd brought with him from his nearby castle. Fleet of foot as one of the goats she so loved, Amélie stole near enough to the miscreants to discover their dire purpose in her beloved land. The count planned to wait until nightfall, then seize control of the Genovian Palace and its populace and add them to his own already sizeable holdings.

'A quick-thinking girl, Amélie hurried back to her flock. The sun was already low in the sky, and Amélie knew she would not be able to return to her village and inform them of the count's dastardly plan until it was far too late and he would already be on the move. And so instead she began to sing one of her plaintive folk tunes, pretending to be oblivious of the scores of hardened soldiers just a few hillocks over . . .

'It was then that a miracle occurred,' Grandmere went on. 'One by one the loathsome mercenaries dropped off, lulled to sleep by Amélie's lilting voice. And when finally the count too sunk into the deepest of slumbers, Amélie scurried back to his side and – taking the little axe she kept with her for cutting away the brambles which often clung to the coats of her beloved goats – she whacked off his head and held it high for his suddenly wakeful army to see.

'"Let this be a warning to anyone who dares to dream of defiling my beloved Genovia,"' Amélie cried, waving the count's lifeless skull.

'And with that the mercenaries – terrified that this small, seemingly defenceless girl was an example of the kind of fighters they would encounter if they set foot on Genovian soil – gathered their things and rode quickly back whence they came. And Amélie, returning to her family with the count's head as proof of her astonishing tale, was quickly hailed the country's saviour and lived long and well in her native land for the rest of her days.'

Then Grandmere reached out and undid a latch on the pendant, causing the thing to spring open and reveal what was nested inside . . .

'And this,' she said all dramatically, 'is all that remains of St Amélie today.'

I looked at the thing inside the locket.

'Um,' I said.

'It's all right, Amelia,' Grandmere said encouragingly. 'You may touch it. It's a right reserved only for the Renaldi royal family. You may as well take advantage of it.'

I reached out and touched whatever was inside the

locket. It looked – and felt – like a rock.

'Um,' I said again. 'Thanks, Grandmere. But I don't know how my touching some saint's rock is supposed to make me feel better.'

'That is no rock, Amelia,' Grandmere said scornfully. 'That's St Amélie's petrified heart!'

EWWWWWWWWWWWWWWWWWWWW!!!!!!!!!!!!!

THIS is what Grandmere busted in here to show me? THIS is how she tries to cheer me up? By having me pick up some dead saint's petrified HEART????

WHY CAN'T I HAVE A NORMAL GRANDMA WHO TAKES ME TO SERENDIPITY FOR FROZEN HOT CHOCOLATE WHEN I'M DOWN instead of making me fondle petrified body parts??????

And, OK, I GET it. I GET that I'm named after a woman who performed an incredible act of bravery and saved her country. I GET what Grandmere was trying to do: instil some of St Amélie's chutzpah into me in time for my big debate against Lana tomorrow.

But I'm afraid her plan totally backfired, because the truth is, except for a fondness for goats, Amélie and I have NOTHING in common. I mean, sure, Rocky stops crying when I sing to him. But it's not like anybody's rushing out to make me a saint.

Also, I highly doubt St Amélie's boyfriend was all 'I'm not going to wait around forever'. Not if she still had that meat cleaver on her.

It's all just so depressing. I mean, even my own grandmother thinks I can't beat Lana Weinberger without divine intervention. That is just so nice.

Oh great. Time to go home.

Sunday, September 6, 9 p.m., the Loft

I'm sooooooooo glad to be back. It feels like I've been gone for SO MUCH LONGER than just two days. Seriously. It feels like a YEAR since I last lay on this bed with Fat Louie curled around my feet, purring his head off, and the dulcet tones of Lash in my ears, since I don't have to listen for Rocky's mournful cry because my mom cured him of the crying-to-get-attention thing. Apparently she did it by leaving him with Mamaw and Papaw to babysit while she and Mr G went to a classic-car show in the parking lot of the Kroger Sav-on, because that was the closest thing to a cultural event that was actually going on in Versailles this past weekend.

By the time they got home – four hours later – Mamaw and Papaw were still sitting exactly where they'd been when Mom and Mr G had left (in front of the TV, watching *America's Funniest Home Videos*) and Rocky was sound asleep. All Mamaw said was, 'Well, he's got a set of lungs on him, I'll say that fer'im.'

Anyway Mom says Mr G was a real trooper, and that if she hadn't been sure he loved her before she definitely knows it now, because no other man would willingly have put up with as many indignities as he endured on her behalf, one of which included riding on Papaw's tractor (Mr G says the closest to a tractor he's ever been on before is the Zamboni at a Rangers game). Mr G says he was particularly impressed by the road signs he saw along the highway from Indianapolis Airport, urging him to repent his sins and be saved. Although he reports that sadly the Versailles County Bank appears to have taken down the 'If bank is closed, please slide money under the door' sign I loved so much.

I was very pleased to hear that they followed all of my advice and kept Rocky far away from hay threshers, copperhead snakes and Hazel, Mamaw's goat. Mom did say something about how it wasn't actually necessary for me to have called every three hours to let them know that there was no cyclone activity on Doppler Radar in their area, but that she appreciated my sisterly vigilance on Rocky's behalf.

Later, while Mr G was struggling to fit their suitcases back into the crawlspace, I asked Mom if she'd happened to look up Wendell Jenkins and she was all, 'Why would I?'

'Because,' I said. 'I mean, you loved him.'

'Sure,' Mom said. 'Twenty years ago.'

'Yeah,' I said. 'But you loved Dad fifteen years ago and you see still see *him*.'

'Because I have a child with him,' my mom said, looking at me sort of strangely. 'Believe me, Mia, if it weren't for you, your dad and I probably wouldn't have anything to do with each other. We've both moved on, just like Wendell and I moved on.'

Then my mom said, 'If I hadn't met Frank, maybe I'd regret breaking up with Wendell or your dad. But I'm married to the man of my dreams. So in answer to your question, Mia, no, I didn't look up Wendell Jenkins this weekend.'

Wow. That is just . . . I don't know. So *nice*. About Mr G being the man of my mom's dreams. I mean, I hope he realizes it. How lucky he is. Because whereas I strongly suspect there are a lot of women out there who might consider my dad, being a rich prince and all, the man of *their* dreams, I don't think there are a whole lot of ladies who are going, 'Hmmm, I wish I could meet a poor, flannel-shirt wearing, drum-playing

Algebra teacher named Frank Gianini,' like my mom evidently did.

Anyway that's kind of nice. That both my mom and I are with the men of our dreams at the same time . . .

Except that mine is about to break up with me.

But would the man of my dreams REALLY tell me he's not going to wait around for me forever? Wouldn't the man of my dreams be willing to wait around for all ETERNITY to have me? I mean, look at Tom Hanks in the movie *Castaway*. He TOTALLY waited for Helen Hunt. For FOUR years.

And OK, it's not like he had much of a choice since there weren't exactly any other girls running around on that island with him, but whatever.

Anyway when I got home I found a message from Michael on the answering machine. It was almost exactly like the one he'd left for me at the hotel, asking me to call.

And when I turned on my computer there was an email from him, too, saying basically the same thing he'd said in both phone messages: to call him.

No way am I falling for that one. I'm not calling him just so he can break up with me.

Ooooooo nooooooooo, Instant Message!

Let it be Michael.

No, don't let it be Michael.

Let it be Michael.

No, don't let it be Michael.

Let it be Michael.

No, don't let it be Michael.

Let it be Michael.

Iluvromance:Hey! It's me!

Oh. It's Tina.

```
FtLouie:    Hi, T.
>
Iluvromance:Just wanted to say thanx again for
            the GR8 time on Friday nite. It was
            SO MUCH fun.
>
FtLouie:    OK. Thanks.
>
Iluvromance:Hey, what's the matter?
>
FtLouie:    Nothing.
>
Iluvromance:SOMETHING  is  the  matter.  You
            haven't used a single exclamation
            point yet! What's wrong? Did you and
            Michael have The Talk?
```

Sometimes I think Tina must be psychic.

```
FtLouie:    Yes. And, Tina, it was AWFUL. He
            totally shot down the idea of doing
            it on prom night and says he can't
            afford the Four Seasons. He was
            nowhere NEAR as nice as Boris about
            it. He even said he wasn't going to
            wait around for me forever!!!!!!!!!
>
Iluvromance:NO! He did NOT say that!!!!
>
FtLouie:    He totally did!!! Tina, I don't know
            what to do. My world is collapsing
```

around me. It's like Lana was
TOTALLY RIGHT.

>

Iluvromance: That is not possible, Mia. You must
have misunderstood.

>

FtLouie: Believe me, I didn't. Michael wants
to Do It and isn't going wait around
forever for me to make up my mind
about it either. I can't believe
this. All this time, you know, I
thought he was the man of my dreams!!

>

Iluvromance: Mia, Michael IS the man of your
dreams. But just because you've
found your one true love doesn't
mean that your relationship isn't
going to be fraught with hardship
from time to time.

>

FtLouie: It doesn't?

>

Iluvromance: Oh, gosh, no! The road to romantic
bliss is filled with many potholes
and speed bumps. People think that
once they've found that special
someone everything is smooth sailing. But nothing could be further
from the truth. Good relationships
only stay that way through hard work
and personal sacrifice on the part
of both participants.

>

FtLouie: Then . . . what should I do?
>
Iluvromance:Well . . . I don't know. How did you
            leave things?
>
FtLouie: Um, Lars banged on the door and said
            it was time for me to go home. And
            I haven't spoken to Michael since.
>
Iluvromance:Well, what are you doing sitting
            there, writing to ME? Get on the
            phone and call Michael right now!!!
>
FtLouie: You really think I should?
>
Iluvromance:I KNOW you should. Let him know how
            much you love him and how hard this
            is for you and how much you're hurt-
            ing inside. Then TALK to him, Mia.
            Remember, communication is the key.
>
FtLouie: Well, if you really think it'll
            help, I guess I could—
>
WomynRule: Hey, Mia. So tomorrow's the big day.
            Are you ready?
>
FtLouie: Lilly, where have you been? Your
            mother was looking for you. You
            haven't been messing around with
            those nuns again, have you? You know
            Sergeant McLinsky told you to leave
            them alone.

>

WomynRule: For your information, little missy,
I have spent the entire day working
tirelessly on YOUR behalf. You are
going to ACE that debate tomorrow,
thanks to some info I was just able
to independently confirm. Although
one of these days I WILL bring those
nuns down. They are up to no good
in there, of THAT I can assure you.

>

FtLouie: Lilly, what are you talking about?
What info? And your mother wants you
to walk Pavlov.

>

WomynRule: Already done. Hey, are you and my
brother in a fight or something?

>

FtLouie: WHY???? DID HE ASK ABOUT ME????

>

WomynRule: Well, that answers THAT question.
And yes, he did ask if I'd heard
from you. But right now I want you
to put whatever personal differences
you're having with my brother OUT OF
YOUR MIND. I need you to be at your
best tomorrow for the BIG DEBATE. Go
to bed early tonight — like right
now, for instance — and eat a really
good breakfast in the morning. AND
THINK POSITIVE. There's an abbreviated fourth period tomorrow, with an
assembly in the gym for the debate.

Then voting's right after, at lunch. NO PRESSURE. But if you don't do well at the debate everything we've done so far — the posters, the networking at the soccer game, all of it — will have been for nothing.

>

FtLouie: NO PRESSURE??? Lilly, I'm under NOTHING BUT pressure!!!! The country over which I will one day rule is being kicked out of the EU. My grandmother made me touch a dead saint's petrified heart. My boyfriend wants to Do It. My baby brother doesn't need to be sung to any more—

>

WomynRule: My brother wants to WHAT???????

>

FtLouie: OMG. I didn't mean to admit that.

>

WomynRule: YOU CAN'T DO IT BEFORE I DO IT!!! I WILL KILL YOU!!!!

>

FtLouie: I AM NOT DOING IT. YET. I said he WANTS to Do It. Someday.

>

WomynRule: Oh God. Then what's the problem? ALL guys want to Do It, you should know that by now. Just tell him to cool his jets.

>

FtLouie: You can't tell someone like your brother to cool his jets, Lilly. He is a MANLY man and has a manly man's needs. You wouldn't tell BRAD PITT to cool his jets. No. Because BRAD PITT is a manly man. LIKE YOUR BROTHER.

>

WomynRule: OK, only you, Mia, would call my brother a manly man. But whatever. Don't think about all that tonight. Tonight just concentrate on getting a good night's sleep, so you can be fresh for the debate tomorrow morning. And don't worry. You're gonna knock 'em dead.

>

FtLouie: LILLY!!! WAIT!!! I CAN'T DO IT!!! THE DEBATE, I MEAN!!! YOU HAVE TO DO IT FOR ME!!! YOU'RE THE ONE WHO WANTS TO BE PRESIDENT ANYWAY!!!!!!!! I HAVE A FEAR OF PUBLIC SPEAKING!!!! NONE OF THE GREAT WOMEN OF GENOVIA HAS BEEN GOOD IN FRONT OF CROWDS!!! WE'RE ONLY GOOD AT KILLING MA-RAUDERS!!! LILLY!!!!!!!!!!!!

>

WomynRule: terminated
>

Iluvromance:If it's any consolation to you, Mia, I think you'll do great tomorrow.

>

FtLouie: Thanks, Tina. But I have to go now. I think I'm going to be sick.

Monday, September 7, 1 a.m.

I cannot do this. I canNOT do this. I am going to make the hugest fool of myself . . .

Why did I ever say I would do this?

Monday, September 7, 3 a.m.

This isn't fair. Haven't I endured enough for one person in my lifetime? Why must total humiliation in front of my peers – once again – be added to it?

Monday, September 7, 5 a.m.

Why won't Fat Louie stop sleeping on my head?

Monday, September 7, 7 a.m.

I'm going to die now.

Monday, September 7, Homeroom

Really, if you think about it, I'm worrying for nothing. I mean, if the world really is going to end in ten to twenty years due to all of the accessible petroleum running out, you have to ask yourself, What's the big deal?

And what about the ice caps melting? If that happens New York won't even exist any more.

And the supervolcano in Yellowstone? Hello, nuclear WINTER.

And what about the killer algae? If my snails don't work, the entire Mediterranean coast will be destroyed. It's really only a matter of time before every sea-floor in the entire world is carpeted with *Caulerpa taxifolia*. Life as we know it will cease, because there will no longer be any seafood . . . no shrimp scampi or lobster rolls or smoked salmon . . . since there won't be any shrimp or lobster or salmon. Or anything else living in the ocean. Except killer algae.

Really, considering all of this, isn't my debate with Lana just SLIGHTLY insignificant?

Monday, September 7, PE

WHY did we have to start our section on volleyball today of all days? I SUCK at volleyball. All that smacking the ball with the insides of your wrists . . . it really HURTS! I am totally going to have black-and-blue marks.

And also I don't appreciate Mrs Potts's little joke of making Lana and me team captains. Because, of course, it totally descended into a game of the Popular versus the Unpopular, with Lana picking Trisha and all of her heinous friends, and me picking Lilly and all of the uncoordinated rejects in the class on account of, well, I knew LANA wasn't going to pick them and I didn't want them to feel left out, because I KNOW what it's like to be the last person picked for a team. It's the most horrible feeling in the world, standing there while the person doing the picking flicks a glance your way then moves coolly past you as if you weren't even THERE!

And, of course, Lana won the coin toss, so she got to serve first and she whacked that ball straight AT ME, I swear. Good thing I ducked or it might have hit me and left a bruise.

And I don't care if Mrs Potts DOES say that's the point. Hasn't she heard of all those volleyball-related injuries that occur every year? How would SHE like to have an EYE put out by a BALL?

But then none of my teammates rushed forward to hit it because clearly ALL of them knew the volleyball-to-eye-related-injury ratio as well as I did.

Needless to say we lost every round.

Now Lana is prancing around the locker room in Ramon Riveras's soccer shorts, talking about what a

FABULOUS time they had this weekend after the game. Apparently she and Ramon went sailing around Manhattan on her dad's yacht. This is something she won't be able to do when the ice caps melt, because Manhattan won't exist any more since it will be under water, so I hope she appreciated it. Although I don't think she did because she said they had a fun time throwing bottle caps overboard and watching the sea-gulls swoop down to try to eat them, not realizing they were bottle caps and not food.

Obviously Lana is not very environmentally savvy if she doesn't realize those bottle caps could choke a not particularly intelligent seagull or fish.

Then her dad took them to the Water Club, a restaurant I have always wanted to go to, but which will probably be going out of business soon if some-thing isn't done about the killer algae strangling all the other undersea plant life in the world.

Although I highly doubt that Lana has ever once in her life thought about what's going on UNDER the ocean. She only cares about what's going on ON TOP of the water. As in how she looks in a bikini.

Which, having seen her in a thong, I can honestly state is disgustingly good.

But that doesn't make her a good person.

Why won't someone shoot me?

Monday, September 7, Geometry

Two more periods until I make a fool of myself in front of the entire school.

Indirect proof = assumption made at the beginning that leads to contradiction. Contradiction indicates the assumption is false and the desired conclusion is true.

Because Lana is pretty, she must be nice. Because all things that are pretty are nice.
FALSE FALSE FALSE FALSE.
Killer algae is pretty, but it is also deadly.

Postulate = a statement that is assumed to be true without proof.
I can pretty much postulate that I will lose today's debate to Lana.

You know what? I think I might be getting the hang of this Geometry thing.
Oh my God, wouldn't it be weird if all this time I thought I was good at one thing and bad at another, and it turns out I was really bad at that one thing and good at another????
Except . . . I don't want to be a mathematician when I grow up. I want to be a WRITER. I want to be good at WRITING. I don't WANT to be good at Geometry.
Well, OK, I want to be good at it. Just not, you know, SO good that I start winning all these Geometry prizes and everyone is all, 'Mia! Mia! Solve this theorem!'
Because that would be boring.

Monday, September 7, English

One more period until I make a fool of myself in front of the entire school.

Look at her. Who does she think she is, in those Samantha Chang slippers?

I know! She fully thinks she's all that. You can so tell.

I bet she doesn't even need those glasses. She probably just wears them to distract from the fact that she has horrible, squinty little eyes.

Totally. And those cargo pants. Hello.

SO last year. I think.

MIA!!! ARE YOU PUMPED???? You don't look pumped. In fact you look as crappy as you did in PE. Did you get ANY sleep at all last night?

How was I supposed to sleep, knowing, as I did, that today I'm going to flayed alive in front of the entire student body — like that guy in *Horatio Hornblower*?

Nobody is going to get flayed alive. Except maybe Lana. Because you are going to flatten her.

LILLY! I'm NOT! I'm no good at public speaking, you KNOW that. And evolutionarily speaking, Lana has the advantage of both looks AND the fact that her socio-political group is the one to whom the rest of us willingly tithe.

What are you talking about?

Just trust me. I'm going to lose.

You aren't. I have a secret weapon.

YOU'RE GOING TO SHOOT HER?????

No, Tina, you FREAK, I am not going to shoot Lana during the debate. I have a little something up my sleeve that — if the student body looks unconvinced — I will pull out. But only if Mia looks as if she needs it.

I NEED IT!!!! I NEED IT!!!!

Patience, my young Padawan.

Lilly, PLEASE, if you know something you've got to tell me, I'm DYING here. Between your brother and this and the snails, I'm completely fried—

Mia! She wants to see you! In the hallway!

Breathe. Just breathe. And you'll be all right.
Just like Drew in *EVER AFTER*.

That's easy for you to say, Lilly. She didn't stomp all over YOUR dreams.

Monday, September 7, third-floor stairwell

Who does she think she is? I mean, REALLY? Does she think just because I'm BLONDE (well, OK, dishwater blonde, but still) and a PRINCESS that I'm STUPID too?

If so, she's going to have to WORK ON THAT POSTULATE.

'Mia,' she said, after dragging me out into the hallway 'so we can talk' in front of EVERYONE. 'I've spoken with your father. He came in on Friday to talk to me about your schoolwork. Mia, I had no idea you were so upset over your grades in my class. You should have said something . . .'

Um, hello, I believe I did. I asked to rewrite the paper. Remember, Ms Martinez?

'. . . you know you can come talk to me about anything, anytime.'

Um, oh, OK. Can I talk to you about how Justin just needs to get over it and take Britney back because this little fight between the two of them has gone on long enough? No, I don't believe I can, can I, Ms Martinez? Because you don't like slick popular-culture references.

'I know I'm a harsh grader, Mia, but really, a B is very good for my class. I've only given out one A so far this semester.'

Um, I know, because I saw it. On *Lilly's* writing sample.

'The only reason I didn't feel comfortable giving you an A is because I still don't think you're working up to your potential. You're a very talented writer, Mia, but you need to apply yourself and stick to topics that are a little more substantive than Britney Spears.'

THIS is what's wrong with this school. That people

don't understand that Britney Spears IS a substantive topic! She is a human barometer by which the mood of the country can be determined. When Britney does something outrageous people reach excitedly for their copy of *US Weekly* and *In Touch* magazine. Britney gives us all something exciting to look forward to. Yes, there might be murders and natural disasters and other downers in the news. But then there's Britney, French kissing Madonna on the MTV Music Video Awards, and suddenly things don't seem quite so bad as they did before.

I guess my outrage must have shown on my face because, a second later, Ms Martinez was all, 'Mia? Are you all right?'

But I didn't say anything. Because what COULD I say?

Great. The late bell for fourth period just went off. I'm going to get a tardy from Mademoiselle Klein when I finally get to French.

Not that I care. What's a tardy compared to what's going to happen to me in precisely forty minutes in front of the WHOLE SCHOOL?

Monday, September 7, French

0 periods until I make a fool of myself in front of the entire school.

WHERE WERE YOU???? YOU MISSED IT!!!!

Missed what? What are you talking about, Shameeka? WAIT – Did everybody circle around Perin and chant 'PULL DOWN YOUR PANTS'????

Of course not. But Mademoiselle Klein DID make us all read our histoires *out loud, and we had to say our name first when we did it – you know, like* 'Mon histoire, par Shameeka' *and when we got to Perin, who said,* 'Mon histoire, par Perinne,' *Mademoiselle Klein went,* 'You mean Perin,' *and Perin went,* 'No, Perinne,' *and Mademoiselle Klein went,* 'No, you mean Perin because Perin is the masculine for Perin and you're a boy. Perinne is feminine,' *and Perin went,* 'I know Perinne is feminine. I'M A GIRL.'

PERIN IS A GIRL???? OH MY GOD!!!!! Poor Perin! How embarrassing! I mean, that Mademoiselle Klein thought he was a he. I mean, that she was a he. Well, you know what I mean. What did she do? Mademoiselle Klein, I mean?

Well, she apologized of course. What else COULD she do? Poor Perin turned BRIGHT RED. I felt so sorry for her!

That's OK, Shameeka. We'll ask him – or her – to sit with us at lunch today. I saw him – her – sitting by herself all last week, over by the guy who hates it when they put corn in the chilli. I really think she needs us.

Oh! That's such a good idea! You're so good at things like that. Knowing how to make people feel better. It's kind of like—

What?

Well, I was going to say it's kind of like you're a princess, or something. But you ARE a princess! So of course you're good at that kind of thing. It's kind of like your job.

Yeah. It kind of is, isn't it?

Monday, September 7, Principal Gupta's office

You know what? I don't even care. I don't even care that I'm sitting here in the principal's office.

I don't care that Lana is sitting here beside me, shooting me evil looks.

I don't care that the lion-head badge is hanging off my blazer by a few threads.

And I don't care that the entire school is currently in the gym, waiting for us to arrive for our debate.

Where does she get off? That's what I want to know. Lana, I mean. HOW DARE SHE??? It is one thing to pick on me, but it is QUITE another to pick on someone who is completely defenceless, not to mention NEW TO OUR SCHOOL.

If she thinks I'm going to stand idly by and just let her make fun of someone that way, she is sadly, sadly mistaken. Well, I suppose she realizes that, seeing as how I'm still holding a chunk of her hair. Although I guess it's not actually her hair since it turned out to be a clip-on extension braid she'd added to show her school spirit (it's a blue ribbon braided into a lock of fake blonde hair).

Which would explain why it came out so easily in my hand when I lunged at her, intent on ripping out every strand of hair on her stupid head, after she told me to mind my own business and ripped off my AEHS Lion sew-on patch.

Still. I hope it hurt.

The sad thing is she doesn't know how lucky she is. I'd have inflicted a lot more damage if Lars and Perin hadn't held me back.

Perin may have turned out to be a girl, but she's a surprisingly strong one.

She's also very well-mannered. As Principal Gupta was dragging me off to her office I heard Perin call, 'Thank you, Mia!'

And although I may be mistaken in this – I was still in a rage-fuelled frenzy – I think a few people even applauded.

Except, of course, it would never occur to Principal Gupta that *Lana* might have done anything wrong. Please! She thinks the reason I lunged at Lana was 'nerves' over the debate. Yeah, that's right, Principal Gupta. It was nerves all right. It had NOTHING to do with the fact that as we were coming out of French Lana walked by and leaned over to Perin and said, 'HERMAPHRODITE.'

Or that I, in response, told Lana to shut her stupid mouth.

Or that Lana, in retaliation, reached out and yanked off my AEHS Lion patch.

The part where I, totally instinctively, yanked off Lana's clip-on braid was the only part Principal Gupta heard about.

Principal Gupta says I'm lucky she doesn't suspend me on the spot. She says the only reason she's not is because she knows I have a lot of problems at home right now. (HELLO??? WHAT IS SHE TALKING ABOUT? THE SNAILS? THE FACT THAT I'M A BABY-LICKER? THAT MY BOYFRIEND WANTS TO DO IT SOMEDAY? WHAT?????)

She says she thinks it would be better for Lana and me to take out our differences with one another in a more civilized manner than brawling in the second-floor hallway. She's making us go through with the debate after all. She says, 'Mia, will you please lift your head out of that journal and pay attention to what I'm saying?'

Jeez. What does she THINK I'm writing about? *Star Wars* fan fic?

Lana's laughing of course.

I don't think she'd be laughing quite so hard if she found out that I happen to be named after someone who cut off another person's head with a meat cleaver.

Monday, September 7, the gym

Oh God. How did I ever get into this? They're ALL here. All 1,000 students at Albert Einstein High School, grades nine through twelve, sitting there in the bleachers in front of me, LOOKING at me, STARING at me, because there's nothing else to stare at, except for Lana and the two podiums and this potted palm they pulled out to make it look homier or something – or maybe to provide me with oxygen if I start to pass out – and Principal Gupta, standing in between our two folding chairs like a referee at a prize fight.

I'm totally going to barf into the potted palm.

Principal Gupta is going on about how this is just a friendly debate so that Lana and I can let the voters know where we stand on the issues.

Friendly. Right. That's why I'm still holding Lana's braid in my hand.

And hello, issues? There are ISSUES???? NOBODY TOLD ME THERE WERE GOING TO BE ISSUES!!!

I can see Lilly, her video camera pointed and ready, in the front row of bleachers – sitting with Tina and Boris and Shameeka and Ling Su and, oh look, isn't that sweet, Perin – signalling me. What is Lilly trying to tell me? She can't be getting ready to pull out her secret weapon. Not yet anyway. The debate hasn't even started! What is she doing with her hands??? Why is she making that folding motion?

Oh, I get it. She wants me to sit up straight and stop writing in my journal. Yeah, fat chance, Lilly. I—

OH MY GOD. That smell. I recognize that smell. Chanel Number Five. Only one person I know of wears Chanel Number Five – or at least slathers on so much

227

of it that you can smell it from miles off before she even enters the room.

WHAT IS SHE DOING HERE????

Oh God. Why ME? Seriously. They should NOT allow people's families to just saunter on to school grounds whenever they feel like it. I would not have half the amount of problems I currently have if there were some kind of security at this school, keeping my parents and grandparents OUT of it.

Oh no. Not my dad too.

And Rommel.

Yes. My grandmother brought her DOG to my debate.

And a phalanx of reporters.

Good grief? Is that LARRY KING????

Great. All I need now is for my mom and Rocky to show up, and it'll turn into a Thermopolis-Gianini-Renaldo family reunion—

Oh. And there she is. Waving Rocky's little arm at me from the bleachers. Hi, Rocky! So glad you could come! So glad you could come watch your sister be totally and systematically annihilated by her mortal enemy—

Oh no. It's starting.

WHERE IS MICHAEL WHEN I NEED HIM????

Monday, September 7, ladies' room

Well, here I am. In the ladies' room. How unusual.

I don't think I'll be coming out for a while. A long, long while. As in . . . maybe never.

The whole thing was so surreal. I mean, I saw Principal Gupta tap on the microphone. I heard the murmuring from the people in the bleachers suddenly stop. Every single eye in the place was on us.

And then Principal Gupta welcomed everyone to the debate – making a special effort to thank Larry King for coming, with his cameras – and explained the importance of the Student Council and the vital role the President plays in its governance. Then she said, 'We have two very different young ladies – each with her own uniquely, er, *strong* personality – running for office today. I hope you will give them all your attention while each of our candidates tells us why she is suited to the role of President, and what she intends to do to make Albert Einstein High School a better place.'

And then – I guess as punishment for the whole braid-ripping-out thing – Principal Gupta let Lana go first.

The applause that went up as Lana swished her way to her podium could only be called thunderous. The whoops and catcalls, the chants of 'La-na, La-na', were almost deafening, especially since it was the gym, after all, and the sound really carried, what with the metal rafters.

Then Lana – looking coolly unconcerned over the fact that she was addressing 1,000 of her peers and another seventy-five or so members of the AEHS faculty and staff (if you count the lunch ladies), my entire family and a number of CNN correspondents – began to speak.

Suffice it to say that what those 1,000 peers of hers

wanted to hear – well, most of them anyway – Lana gave them. Not surprisingly Lana turned out to be a strong supporter of better cafeteria food, a longer lunch hour, larger mirrors in the girls' bathrooms, less homework, more sports, guaranteed admission from the guidance office to such Ivy League schools as AEHS graduates might want to attend, and more diet and low-carb options in the candy and soda machines. She was against the outdoor security cameras and vowed to have them removed. She promised a cheering student populace that if they elected her as President she would make all of these things happen . . .

. . . even though I happen to know that she can't. Because those security cameras may infringe upon the rights of the people who like to smoke outside the school and litter the steps with their gross cigarette butts, but mostly they help keep the school safe from vandalism and break-ins.

And the food distributor for the cafeteria is the same one who services all the schools and hospitals in the area, and offers the lowest prices for the highest-quality food that can be found in the Tri-State area.

And, if the trustees approve a longer lunch period, they'll have to shorten classes, which are already only fifty minutes.

And where does Lana think she's going to get the money for bigger mirrors in the ladies' room? And has she considered the fact that:

- less homework will leave us less prepared for the college courses some of us might want to take later on?
- more sports will result in less money for enrichment programmes in the arts?

- no one can be guaranteed admission to an Ivy League school, not even people whose parents went there?
- our choices in the candy and soda machines are limited to what the vendors are able to offer?

Obviously not.

But I guess that didn't matter to her. Or to her constituents, since by the time she finished they were screaming their heads off and pounding their feet on the bleachers to show their approval. I saw Ramon Riveras stand up and whip his school blazer around his head a few times to pump up the crowd even more.

Principal Gupta looked a little tight-lipped as she stepped up to the microphone and said, 'Er, um, thank you, Lana. Mia, would you like to respond?'

I thought I was going to barf. I really did. Although I don't know what I possibly could have thrown up, since I hadn't been able to eat breakfast this morning, and only had five Starbursts Lilly had given me, half a Bit-O-Honey mooched off Boris, three Tic Tacs from Lars and a Coke in my system.

But as I started walking towards that podium – my knees shaking so badly I'm surprised they even managed to hold me up – something happened. I don't know what exactly. Or why.

Maybe it was the intermittent booing.

Maybe it was the way Trisha Hayes pointed at my combat boots and snickered.

Maybe it was the way Ramon Riveras cupped his hands over his mouth and shouted, '*PIT! PIT!*' in a manner that could hardly be called flattering.

But as I looked out at the sea of humanity before me

and saw bobbing amidst it Perin's bright and shining face as she clapped her guts out for me, it was like the ghost of my ancestress Rosagunde, the first princess of Genovia, took over my body.

Either that or my patron saint, Amélie, did some swooping down from the clouds to lend me some of her meat-cleavering attitude.

In any case even though I still wanted to barf and all, when I got to the podium and remembered the way Grandmere had harangued me about leaning my elbows on it I did something totally unheard of in the history of Student Council presidential debates at Albert Einstein High School.

I ripped the microphone off its stand and, holding it in my hand, went to stand in FRONT of the podium.

Yeah. In front. So there was nothing for me to shield my body behind.

Nowhere for me to hide.

Nothing separating me from my audience.

And then, when they fell into a stunned silence because of this unusual move, I said – not having the slightest idea where the sudden tide of words flowing from me was coming from:

'"Give me your tired, your poor/Your huddled masses yearning to breathe free." That's what it says on the Statue of Liberty. That's the first thing millions of immigrants to this country saw when they stepped on to its shores. A statement assuring them that into this great melting pot of a nation, *all* would be welcome, regardless of socio-economic status, what colour hair she has, whom she might be dating, whether she waxes, shaves or goes au naturel, or whether or not she chooses to play a sport.

'And isn't a school a melting pot unto itself? Aren't we a group of people thrown together for eight hours a day, left to fend as best we can?

'But despite the fact that we here at Albert Einstein are a nation unto ourselves, I don't exactly see us acting like one. All I see are a bunch of people who've split off into cliques for their own protection and who are totally afraid to let anybody new – any of the huddled masses yearning to breathe free – into their precious, selective little group.

'Which totally sucks.'

I let this sink in for a minute as before me I saw a ripple of disbelief pass over my audience. Larry King murmured something into Grandmere's ear.

But it was like I didn't even care. I mean, I still felt like projectile vomiting all over the Jocks, who were sitting directly in front of me.

But I didn't. I just kept going. Like . . .

Well, like St Amélie.

'History has tried and rejected many forms of government over time, including governance of divine right, something this country abolished hundreds of years ago.

'And yet for some reason, at this school, the divine right of governance still seems to exist. There's a certain set of people who seem to believe they have an inherent right to office because they are more attractive than the rest of us – or better at sports – or get invited to more parties than we do.'

As I said this, I looked very pointedly back at Lana, then eyed Ramon and Trisha too, for good measure. Then I looked again at the crowd before me, most of whom were staring at me with their mouths open – and not, like Boris, because of deviated septums either.

'These are the people who are at the top of the evolutionary ladder,' I went on. 'The people with the nicest complexions. The people with the bodies that are shaped most like the models we see in magazines. The people who always have the hottest new bag or sunglasses. The popular people. The people who want to make you wish you were more like them.

'But I'm standing here before you today to tell you that I've been there. That's right. I've been to the popular side. And guess what? It's all a scam. These people, who act as if they have a right to govern you and me, are completely unqualified for the job due to the simple fact that they don't believe in the most fundamental precepts of our nation, and that's that we are ALL CREATED EQUAL. Not a single one of us is better than any other person here. And that includes any princesses who might be in the room.'

This got a laugh, even though the truth is, I wasn't trying to be funny. Still, the laugh made me feel a little less like barfing for some reason. I mean . . . I had made people laugh.

And not, you know, AT me. But at something I'd said. And not in a mocking way either.

I don't know. But that felt kind of . . . cool.

And suddenly, even though I could still feel my palms sweating and my fingers shaking, I felt . . . good.

'Look,' I said. 'I am not going to stand up here and promise you a bunch of junk you and I both know I can't deliver.' I looked back at Lana, who had crossed her arms over her chest and now made a face at me. I turned back to the crowd. 'Longer lunch periods? You know the board of trustees will never approve that. More sports? Is there anyone here who really feels his or her sports needs aren't being met?'

A few hands shot up.

'And is there anyone here who feels that his or her *creative* or *educational* needs aren't being met? Anybody who thinks that this school needs a literary magazine, or new digital video, photography and editing technology for the film and photography clubs, or a kiln for the art department, or a new stage-lighting system for the drama club more than it needs another soccer district championship trophy?'

Many, many more hands shot up.

'Yeah,' I said. 'That's what I thought. There is a real problem in this school, and that's that for too long a group that is in the minority has been making decisions for the majority. And that is just *wrong*.'

Someone whooped. And I don't even think it was Lilly.

'Actually,' I said, encouraged by the whoop, 'it's *more* than just wrong. It's a total violation of the principles upon which this nation was founded. As the philosopher John Locke put it, "Government is legitimate only to the extent that it is based on the consent of the people being governed." Are you really going to give your consent to the privileged few to make your decisions for you? Or are you going to entrust those decisions to someone who actually understands you – someone who shares your ideals, your hopes and your dreams? Someone who will do her very best to make sure YOUR voice, and not the voice of the so-called popular minority, is heard?'

At this there was another whoop, and this one came from way on the other side of the bleachers – definitely not one of my friends.

The second whoop was followed by a third. And then there was a smattering of applause. And a voice that shouted, 'Go, Mia!'

Whoa.

'Um, thank you, Mia.' Out of the corner of my eye, I saw Principal Gupta take a step towards me. 'That was very enlightening.'

But I pretended like I hadn't heard her.

That's right. Principal Gupta was giving me the OK to sit down – to get out of the limelight – to shrink back down into my chair.

And I blew her off.

Because I had some more stuff to get off my unendowed chest.

'But that's not all that's wrong with this school,' I said into the microphone, enjoying the way it made my voice bounce around the gym.

'How about the fact that there are people working here – people who call themselves teachers – who seem to feel that theirs is the only legitimate form of expression? Are we really going to tolerate being told by instructors in a field as subjective as something like, oh, English, for example, that the subject matter of our essays is inappropriate because it might be considered – by some – not substantive enough in topical importance? If, for instance, I choose to write a paper about the historical significance of Japanese anime or manga, is my paper worth less than someone else's essay on the caldera in Yellowstone Park that might one day explode, killing tens of thousands of people?

'Or,' I added, as everyone started buzzing because they didn't know that Yellowstone Park is nothing more than a deadly magma reservoir and probably a lot of them have been unknowingly going there on family vacations and whatnot, 'is my paper on Japanese anime or manga

JUST AS IMPORTANT as the paper on the caldera at Yellowstone because knowing, as we do now, that such a caldera exists, we need something entertaining – such as Japanese anime or manga – to get our minds off it?'

There was a moment of stunned silence. Then someone from somewhere in the middle of the bleachers yelled, '*Final Fantasy!*' Someone else yelled, '*Dragonball!*' Another person, from way at the top, shouted, '*Pokémon!*' and got a big laugh.

'Maybe things like the lottery and television were invented to sell products, bilk workers of their hard-earned cash and lull us all into a false sense of complacency, distracting us from the true horrors of the world around us. But maybe we NEED those distractions so that during our leisure time we can enjoy ourselves,' I went on. 'Is there something wrong with, after our work is done, hanging out and watching a little *OC*? Or singing karaoke? Or reading comic books? Does something have to be complicated and hard to understand to be culture? A hundred years from now, after we're all dead from the Yellowstone caldera, or the ice caps melting, or no more petroleum, or killer algae taking over the planet, when whatever remains of human civilization looks back at early-twenty-first-century society, which do you think is going to better describe what our lives were really like – an essay on the ways in which the media exploits us or a single episode of *Sailor Moon*? I'm sorry, but as far as I'm concerned, give me anime or give me death.'

The gym exploded.

Not because the Computer Club had finally succeeded in building a killer robot and setting it loose amongst the cheerleaders.

But because of what I'd said. Really. Because of what

I, Mia Thermopolis, had said.

The thing was, though, I wasn't done.

'So today,' I said, having to shout to be heard over the applause, 'when you're casting your vote for Student Council President, ask yourself this question: What is meant by "the people" in the phrase "governance of the people, by the people"? Does it mean the privileged few? Or the vast majority of us who were born without a silver pom-pom in our mouths? Then vote for the candidate who you feel most represents you, the people.'

And then, my heart slamming into my ribs, I turned, tossed Principal Gupta the microphone and ran from the gym. To thunderous applause.

And into the safety of this bathroom stall.

The thing is I feel so WEIRD. I mean, I have never in my life stood up and done anything like that. Well, except for the parking-meter thing, but that was different. I wasn't asking people to support ME. I was asking them to support less damage to the infrastructure and higher revenue. That was kind of a no-brainer.

This, though.

This was different. I was asking people to put their trust – their vote – in me. Not like in Genovia where that support is kind of automatic because, um, there IS no other princess. It's just me. What I say goes. Or will, you know, when I take over the throne.

Uh-oh. I hear voices in the hallway. The debate must be over. I wonder what Lana said in her rebuttal. I probably should have stuck around to rebut her rebuttal. But I couldn't. I just couldn't.

Oh no. I hear Lilly . . .

Monday, September 7, Gifted and Talented

Well, that was fun. Lunch I mean. Everybody kept stopping by our table to congratulate me and tell me I had their vote. It was kind of cool. I mean, not just people from my clique – the Nerds – but the Sk8terbois and the Punks and the Drama kids and even a few of the Jocks. It was bizarre to be talking to all these people who normally look right past me in the hallway.

And all of a sudden it was like they wanted to sit at MY lunch table for a change.

Only they couldn't, because now that Perin's sitting there, in addition to the regular crowd, there's no more room.

We were a particularly festive bunch today on account of a couple of pieces of good news. At least *I* thought it was good news. And that is that, after I ran from the gym, Lana attempted a rebuttal and she was booed down and couldn't even get a word in edgeways. Principal Gupta had to turn up the sound system until the feedback became so unbearable that people finally calmed down. And by then Lana had left the gym in tears (serves her right. I don't know how I'm going to get my school patch back on. My mom certainly doesn't sew. Maybe I can ask Grandmere's maid).

But that's not the only good thing that happened. After Lilly finally managed to drag me out of the bathroom I ran into my mom and dad and Grandmere. Mom gave me a big hug – and Rocky beamed at me – and told me I'd done her proud.

But Dad had the really big news. He'd heard from the Royal Genovian scuba team, and the *Aplysia depilans* have actually started eating the killer algae! Really and

239

truly! They've already polished off thirty-seven acres practically overnight, and will probably eradicate the entire crop by October, when the waters of the Mediterranean will become too cold to support them and they'll die.

'But that's all right,' Dad said, smiling at me. 'I've already introduced a bill to parliament that calls for another 10,000 snails to be transported to the bay next spring, in case any of our neighbouring country's algae creeps into our territory.'

I could barely believe my ears.

'So does this mean we aren't going to be voted out of the EU?' I asked.

My dad looked shocked.

'Mia,' he said. 'That was never going to happen. Well, I mean, I know a few countries might have *wanted* us ejected from the EU. But I believe they're the same ones who caused this eco-disaster in the first place. So no one was actually giving their calls for our expulsion serious consideration.'

Now he tells me. Nice one, Dad. Like I wasn't up all night, worrying about this. Well, among other things.

It was right about then that I noticed Ms Martinez standing there too, looking kind of . . . well, sheepish is the only way I can think of to describe it.

'Mia,' she said, when I'd finally stopped hugging my dad (in my joy at hearing that my snails had saved the bay). 'I just want to say that that was a great speech. And that you're right. Popular culture isn't necessarily lacking in value or merit. It has its place, just like high culture. I'm very sorry if I made you feel that the things you enjoy writing about were less worthy than more serious subjects. They aren't.'

Whoa!!!!

The fact that my dad was giving Ms Martinez the old eye as all this was going on kind of diminished my joy over my victory somewhat however.

But whatever. I think it's highly unlikely my dad's going to start dating someone who actually knows what a gerund is. His last girlfriend thought gerunds were mean, foul-smelling rodents.

Speaking of which, Grandmere came up to me right after that, took me by the arm and led me a little bit away from everyone.

'You see, Amelia,' she said in a raspy, Sidecar-scented whisper. 'I told you that you could do it. That was inspired in there. Truly inspired. I almost felt as if the spirit of St Amélie was amongst us.'

The freaky thing about this was – I'd kind of felt the same.

But I didn't say so. Instead, I said, 'So, uh, Grandmere? What's this secret weapon you and Lilly came up with? And when are you going to launch it?'

But she just lifted my half-torn-off AEHS patch between her thumb and index finger and said, 'What happened to your coat? Really, Amelia, can't you take better care of your things? A princess really ought not to walk about looking like such a slattern.'

But anyway. The whole thing was still pretty cool. Especially the part where Grandmere said she had to cancel our princess lesson for the day so she could go have a facial at Elizabeth Arden. Apparently, all the stress of helping Lilly with the election has caused her pores to expand.

All in all it was almost enough to make me think things – I don't know – might actually go my way for a change.

But then I remembered Michael. Who, by the way, hasn't once called or even text-messaged me today to say good luck with the debate or ask how I'd done or anything. In fact I haven't talked to him at all since the whole Doing It talk.

And I'll admit, that talk didn't actually go as well as I'd hoped it would.

But still. You'd think he'd call. Even if, you know, I'm the one who hasn't returned HIS calls or emails.

Boris is playing 'God Save the Queen' on his violin on my behalf. I told him it's a little early for that. After all, the votes collected over lunch are still being tabulated. Principal Gupta's going to make the announcement over the loudspeaker last period.

Lilly just went, all softly, to me, 'Then, when you win, next week you can make an announcement of your own. You know, about your stepping down and leaving the presidency to me.'

Huh. Isn't it funny? But up until that moment I had kind of forgotten about that part of our plan.

Monday, September 7, US Government

Mrs Holland congratulated me on my speech today and said it made her proud. PROUD! OF ME!!! A teacher is proud of me!!!

ME!!!!!!!

Monday, September 7, Earth Science

Kenny just said the strangest thing to me. Just blurted it right out as we were drawing our diagrams of the Van Allen radiation belts.

'Mia,' he said. 'I want to tell you something. You know my girlfriend, Heather?'

'Yeeee-ah,' I said reluctantly, because I thought he was getting ready to tell me another long, boring story about Heather's gymnastic prowess.

'Well.' Kenny's face turned as red as the radiation belt I was colouring. 'I made her up.'

!!!!!!!!!!!!!!!!!!!!!!!!

Yes, that is right. Kenny has spent the past seven days telling me MADE-UP stories about his MADE-UP girlfriend, Heather. A girlfriend who, I will admit, I actually felt threatened by! Because she's so perfect! I mean, blonde and sporty AND she gets straight As????

Actually, now that I think about it, I should probably be grateful Heather turns out not to be real. She was making me feel pretty inadequate to tell the truth.

But anyway. I just looked at him and was like, 'Kenny. Why would you do that?'

And he said, all shamefaced, 'I just couldn't stand it, you know? You having this whole perfect princess life, with Michael, your perfect princely boyfriend. It . . . I don't know. It just got to me.'

Yeah. Right. My perfect life. My perfect princess life, with Michael, my perfect princely boyfriend. Let me tell you something, Kenny. You want to know how NOT perfect my perfect princess life is? My perfect princely boyfriend is getting ready to dump me because I don't want to Do It. How's that for perfect, Kenny?

Except, of course, I couldn't say that. Because that's none of Kenny's business. Also because I don't much want the whole Michael-wants-to-Do-It thing getting around school. Thanks to the many movies based – however loosely – on my life that are floating around out there, enough people already think they know everything there is to know about me. I don't need any MORE info leaking out.

But whatever. I just assured Kenny that my life isn't as perfect as he might think. That, in fact, I have a LOT of problems, among them the fact that I am a baby-licker and very nearly got my own country kicked out of the EU.

Surprisingly, this information seemed to cheer him up excessively. So much so, in fact, that I'm feeling kind of annoyed.

Wha—

Oh no. The classroom loudspeaker just crackled. Principal Gupta is coming on to announce the results of today's votes.

Oh God. Oh God. Oh God.

Here it is:

Lana Weinberger, 359 votes.

Mia Thermopolis, 641 votes.

Oh my God.

OH MY GOD.

I'M THE NEW STUDENT COUNCIL PRESIDENT OF ALBERT EINSTEIN HIGH.

Monday, September 7, 5 p.m., Ray's Pizza

OK. That was . . . that was just totally surreal.

I don't even know how else to describe it. I'm in a total and complete daze. Still. And it's been two hours since Principal Gupta declared me the winner. And I've had half a plain-cheese pizza and three Cokes since then.

And I'm STILL in shock.

Maybe it's not so much winning the election as what happened *after* I found out I won the election. Which was . . .

. . . a LOT actually.

First off, everyone in my Earth Science class, including Kenny, started jumping all over the place, congratulating me then asking me if I could please ask the trustees to buy the bio lab an electrophoresis kit, something for which they'd unsuccessfully lobbied the last President.

So, obviously, in no time at all, I understood the full weight of the responsibility I would bear as President.

And . . .

I welcomed it.

I know. I *KNOW*.

I mean, like it's not enough I'm

- the Princess of Genovia
- sister to a defenceless infant whose mother and father are somewhat lacking in the parenting department, if you know what I mean
- a budding writer who still has to get through sophomore Geometry this year
- a teen, with all that that word implies, such as mood swings, insecurities, and the occasional zit

246

- in love with a college boy.

Now I'm actually entertaining the idea of being all that AND President of my school Student Council???

But. Well. Yeah.

Yeah, I am. Because winning that election against Lana?

That totally RULED.

But anyway. That was just the FIRST thing that happened.

The next thing was that after the bell rang, letting us out for the day, I was making my way down to my locker – slowly . . . very slowly, because everyone kept stopping me to congratulate me – when I ran into Lilly, who leaped into my arms (even though I'm a lot taller than she is, she still weighs more. She's lucky I didn't drop her. But I guess I had, like, that adrenaline thing you get when your baby is stuck under a car or you win the presidency of your school's student council or something, since I was able to hold on to her until she climbed down again).

Anyway, Lilly was all, 'WE DID IT!!! WE DID IT!!!!'

And then Tina and Boris and Shameeka and Ling Su and Perin showed up and started jumping up and down along with us. Then we all made our way down to my locker, singing that 'We Are the Champions' song.

Then, as everybody else was chatting excitedly, and I was working the combination to my locker, I noticed something very odd going on at the locker next door to mine. And that was that Ramon Riveras, flanked by Principal Gupta and Lana Weinberger's DAD, of all people, was taking everything – and I do mean EVERYTHING – out of his locker and putting it glumly in his gym bag.

And standing a little way behind him, tears streaming down her face, was Lana, who kept stomping her foot and going, 'But, Daddy, WHY???? Why, Daddy, WHY???'

Except that Dr Weinberger wasn't answering her. He just stood there, looking very solemn, until Ramon had got the last of his stuff out of the locker. Then Principal Gupta said, 'Very well. Come along.'

And she, Ramon, Dr Weinberger and Lana all trailed back to the principal's office.

But not before Lana swung a decidedly nasty look over her shoulder at me and hissed, *'I'll get you back for this if it's the last thing I do! You'll be sorry!'*

I thought she meant she'd get back at me for winning the election over her. But when Shameeka went, 'Hey, where are they taking Ramon?' Lilly smiled in an evil way and said, 'The airport probably.'

While we all asked, in a chorus, what she was talking about, Lilly said, 'My secret weapon. Only after that speech you gave, Mia, I knew we didn't need it. Looks like that grandmother of yours dropped the dime on the Weinbergers anyway, even though she didn't have to. I have to hand it to that Clarisse. She is one old dame you don't want to get on your bad side.'

Since this didn't exactly clear the matter up any – at least as far as I was concerned – I asked Lilly just what the heck she was talking about, and she explained. It turns out that day at the soccer game, when Lilly had been sitting behind Lana's parents, she'd totally eavesdropped on their conversation and found out that Ramon is a wringer!

Yes! He is already a high-school graduate! He graduated last year, back in his native Brazil, where he'd led his school district to claim the national championship!

Dr Weinberger and a couple of the other trustees got the brilliant idea to PAY him to come to this country and enroll at AEHS, so we'd have a chance at actually winning some games for a change.

Lilly and Grandmere had planned on using this information as part of a smear campaign against Lana in the event that it looked as if, after the debate, she was going to win.

But my pulling out *Sailor Moon* and that John Locke quote convinced them I had the election in the bag. So Grandmere ended up not calling Principal Gupta's office to tell her about Ramon until *after* the election results were announced.

I must say this information caused me to look at Lilly in a new light. I mean, I've always known that Lilly is capable of some underhanded things. And I'm not saying the Weinbergers had a right to use poor Ramon that way or to dupe the other trustees.

But, jeez! I would not want to be on the wrong side of Lilly – much less Grandmere – in a fight.

Lilly was standing there, looking all pleased with herself while everyone else patted her on the back and said what a cool thing she had done.

And I guess it *was* cool in a way, if you agree – which I most definitely do – that anything that makes Lana cry is a good thing.

'So,' Lilly said, when I'd got together all my stuff and was standing there, ready to go. 'Since Clarisse let you out of princess hell for the day, want to go celebrate OUR victory?'

She put a very significant emphasis on the word OUR that only a moron would have missed.

I got it all right.

And felt my stomach lurch.

'Um,' I said. 'Yeah, Lilly. About that. Something kind of happened when I was giving that speech today . . .'

'You're telling *me* something happened,' Lilly said, patting me on the back. 'You struck a blow for unpopular kids everywhere, is what happened while you were giving that speech today.'

'Yeah,' I said. 'I know. About that. I just don't know how I feel about it now. I mean, Lilly, don't you think your plan is kind of unfair? Those people voted for *me*. *I'm* the one they expect—'

I saw Lilly's eyes widen at something she saw behind my back.

'What's HE doing here?' she wanted to know. Then, to whoever was standing back there, she said, 'In case you forgot, you GRADUATED, you know.'

Something gripped my heart at her words. Because I knew – just KNEW – who she was talking to.

The LAST person I wanted to see just then.

Or maybe the person I MOST wanted to see just then.

It all depended on what he had to say to me.

Slowly I turned around.

And there stood Michael.

I guess it would sound super dramatic to say that everything else in the hallway seemed to vanish, until it was as if it were only Michael and me alone, standing there, just looking at each other.

If I wrote that in a story, Ms Martinez would probably write CLICHÉ on it or something.

Except that it's NOT a cliché. Because that's really what it was like. Like there was no one else in the whole world except us two.

'We need to talk,' is what Michael said to me. No *Hello*. No *Why didn't you call me?* or *Where have you been?* And certainly no kiss.

Just *We need to talk.*

And those four words were all it took to make my heart feel as shrivelled and hard as St Amélie's.

'OK,' I said, even though my mouth had gone completely dry.

And when he turned around to leave the school, I followed him, after throwing a warning glance over my shoulder – letting Lars know to stay FAR behind me, and Lilly know there wasn't going to be any celebrating.

At least not just yet.

Lars took it like the professional he is. But I heard Lilly scream, 'Fine! Go with your BOYFRIEND! See if we care!'

But Lilly didn't know. Lilly didn't know about how shrivelled and small my heart had suddenly got. Lilly didn't know I suspected that my life – my perfect princess life – was about to explode into fifty billion pieces. That supervolcano under Yellowstone? Yeah, when that thing finally blows, it'll be NOTHING in comparison.

I followed Michael down the steps of the school – right under the watchful eye of the security cameras – and away from the crowds gathered around Joe. I followed him across two avenues, neither of us saying a word. I certainly wasn't going to speak first.

Because everything was different now. If he was going to break up with me because I wouldn't Do It – well, I didn't care.

Oh, I CARED of course. My heart was breaking ALREADY, and all he'd said was, 'We need to talk.'

251

But hello. I am the Princess of Genovia. I am the newly elected President of the AEHS Student Council.

And NO ONE – not even Michael – is going to tell me when to Do It.

Finally we got here – to Ray's Pizza. The place was empty because school hadn't been out long enough for it to fill up, and it was way past lunchtime and not quite dinner.

Michael pointed to a booth and said, 'You want a pie?'

'We need to talk.'

'You want a pie?'

That's all he'd said to me so far.

I said, 'Yes.' And because my mouth still felt as dry as sand, I added, 'And a Coke.'

He went to the counter and ordered both. Then he came back to the booth, slid into the seat across from mine, looked me in the eye and said, 'I saw the debate.'

This was NOT what I'd expected him to say.

It was SO not what I'd expected him to say that my jaw dropped. I didn't remember to shut my mouth again until I felt cool, pizza-scented air on my tongue, and realized I was breathing out of it, just like Boris.

I snapped my mouth shut. Then I asked, 'You were *there?*'

AND YOU DIDN'T COME UP AND SAY HI?????????? Only I didn't say that last part.

Michael shook his head.

'No,' he said. 'It was on CNN.'

'Oh,' I said. Seriously, who else but ME would get their school debate aired on CNN?

And who else but MY BOYFRIEND would happen to catch its broadcast?

'I liked what you said about *Sailor Moon*,' he said.

252

'You DID?' I don't know why this came out so squeaky.

'Yeah. And the John Locke quote? That kicked butt. You get that from Holland's government class?'

I nodded, unable to speak. I was so astonished he'd known this.

'Yeah,' he said. 'She's cool. So.' He leaned an arm against the back of his side of the booth. 'You're the new President of AEHS.'

I folded my hands on the table top, hoping he wouldn't notice the damage I'd done to my fingernails since the last time I'd seen him. Damage that was almost entirely due to worry about HIM.

'Looks like it,' I said.

'I thought Lilly wanted to be President,' Michael said. 'Not you.'

'She does,' I said. 'But now . . . well, I sort of don't want to give it up.'

Michael raised his eyebrows. Then he let out a low whistle.

'Wow,' he said. 'Mind if I'm not around when you explain that to her?'

'No,' I said. 'That's OK.'

Then I froze. Wait . . . if he didn't want to be around when I explained to Lilly that I had no intention of stepping down from the presidency, did that mean . . .

That had to mean that . . .

Suddenly my poor, shrivelled heart seemed to be showing some signs of life.

'Pie's up,' the guy behind the counter said.

So Michael got up and got the pizza and our three sodas – he'd also got one for Lars, who was sitting at a table on the other side of the restaurant, pretending to be very interested in the *Dr Phil* episode the guy behind the counter was watching on the TV hanging from the ceiling – and brought them back to the booth.

I didn't know what else to do. So I pulled a slice from the pie, slapped it on to a paper plate and took it over to Lars, along with his soda. It's no joke, having to worry about your bodyguard all the time.

Then I went and sat back down and pulled my own slice on to a plate and carefully sprinkled hot-pepper flakes all over it.

Michael, as was his custom, merely picked up a slice – seemingly oblivious to the fact that it was steaming hot – folded it in half and took a big bite.

His hands, as he did this, looked alarmingly . . . large. Why had I never noticed this before? How large Michael's hands are?

Then, after he'd swallowed, he said, 'Look. I don't want to fight about this.'

I glanced up at him kind of sharply on account of having been staring at his hands. I wasn't sure what he meant by 'this'. Did he mean about Lilly and the presidency? Or did he mean—

'All I want to know is,' he went on, in a sort of tired voice, 'are we EVER going to Do It?'

OK. Not Lilly and the presidency.

I practically choked on the tiny bite of pizza I'd taken and had to swallow about a gallon of Coke before I was able to say, 'OF COURSE.'

But Michael looked suspicious.

'Before the end of this decade?'

'Absolutely,' I said, with more conviction that I necessarily felt. But, you know. What else could I say? Plus my face was as red as the pizza sauce. I know because I saw my reflection in the napkin holder.

'I knew going into this that it wasn't going to be easy, Mia,' Michael said. 'I mean, aside from the age difference and your being my sister's best friend, there's the whole princess aspect to it . . . the constant-hounding-by-paparazzi/can't-go-anywhere-without-a-bodyguard thing. A lesser man might find all that daunting. I, on the other hand, have always enjoyed a challenge. Besides which, I love you, so it's all worth it to me.'

I practically melted right there on the spot. I mean seriously. Has any guy EVER said anything so sweet?

But then he went on.

'It's not that I'm trying to rush you into something you aren't ready for,' Michael said, as matter-of-factly as if he were discussing the next move he planned on making in Rebel Strike. How do boys do this by the way? 'It's just that I know it takes you a while to get used to things. So I want you to start getting used to this: you're the girl I want. One day, you WILL be mine.'

Now my face was REDDER than the pizza sauce. At least, that's what it felt like.

'Um,' I said. 'OK.' Because what else COULD I say to that????

Besides it wasn't like I was displeased. I WANT Michael to want me.

It's just, you know, for him to SAY it like that was actually kind of . . . I don't know.

Hot.

'So long as that's clear,' Michael said.

'Crystal,' I said, after I'd choked for a while.

Then he said as far as Doing It went, I was off the hook for the time being, but he expected periodic re-evaluation of our stances on that issue.

I asked how often he thought we should re-evaluate

our stances, and he said about once a month, and I said I thought six-month evaluations might be better, and then he said two, and I said three, and then he said, 'Deal.'

Then he got up and went to offer Lars another slice and got sucked into a conversation Lars is having with the guy behind the counter about the Yankees chances in the World Series this year even though, to my knowledge, Michael has never watched a baseball game in his life.

He did, however, design a computer model in which you can input all the statistics concerning a team and it will then tell you what their chances are of beating another team to within a six-point spread.

The fact is, I love him. He's the boy I want. And one day, he WILL be mine.

And now he wants to know if I want to go get a gelato.

I said, 'I most certainly do.'

Ten out of Ten

Princess Amelia Mignonette Grimaldi Thermopolis Renaldo (Mia)

invites you to an exclusive event to celebrate her 18th birthday and the FABULOUS last ever instalment of The Princess Diaries

Dress code: Glamorous and gorgeous. Tiaras optional. And, Lana Weinberger, don't forget your underwear!

Etiquette: No curtsying. No paps. No kissing Prince William.

Mia's princess training is almost over. She can climb out of a limo as elegantly as any European heir presumptive. Even Grandmere approves of her practically perfect boyfriend, J.P. So this is the final instalment, the very end, the last EVER entry in The Princess Diaries. After all, Mia's about to turn eighteen – it's time to leave childish things behind. Like:

1. Lying.
2. Therapy with Dr Knutz – Mia's so ready to move on!
3. Being Albert Einstein High's last and only unicorn*.
4. Thinking about Michael Moscovitz. I mean, come ON. He's in Japan. And, besides, Mia is TOTALLY in love with J.P.
5. Michael who?

* You have *so* got to read the book!

Meg Cabot

air head

meg cabot

She's a brainiac trapped inside the body of an airhead . . .

Teenagers Emerson Watts and Nikki Howard have nothing in common. Em's a tomboy-brainiac who couldn't care less about her looks. Nikki's a stunning supermodel, the world's most famous airhead. But a freak accident causes the girls' lives to collide in the most extraordinary way – and suddenly Em knows more about Nikki's life than the paparazzi ever have!

The first book in a spectacular romantic trilogy with a spine-tingling twist!

ABANDON

MEG CABOT

PIERCE KNOWS WHAT IT'S LIKE TO DIE.

Last year she flatlined following an accident.

During that time Pierce saw a dark world and met a mysterious, irresistible boy.

Now that boy, John Hayden, has turned up at school. Every time she sees him Pierce finds herself in terrible danger. Yet she's still drawn to him.

John wants to take her back to the place she fears the most: the Underworld.

The question is, why?